T0117085

It's time to heal the church to heal the world

by

Jenny Hagemeyer

iUniverse, Inc.
New York Bloomington

Touch Me

It's time to heal the church to heal the world

iUniverse books may be ordered through booksellers or by contacting:

iUniverse
1663 Liberty Drive
Bloomington, IN 47403
www.iuniverse.com
1-800-Authors (1-800-288-4677)

ISBN: 978-1-4401-7778-1 (pbk)
ISBN: 978-1-4401-7779-8 (ebook)

Cover Art Interpretation
"Seasons of Life"
Artist: Fred Hagemeyer
(Belleville, PA 2009)

Printed in the United States of America

iUniverse rev. date: 11/5/2009

Cover Art Interpretation
“Seasons of Life”
Artist: Fred Hagemeyer
(Belleville, PA 2009)

I had been praying for someone to design the front cover of this book. One morning I walked upstairs and noticed a painting that was created by my husband. I realized Fred had been inspired by the Holy Spirit to paint this picture.

The cover depicts a silhouette lifting hands to touch God! When your hand is lifted in Worship to our Almighty God the focus is placed on Him and not your problems.

Living in Pennsylvania we experience all four seasons. My favorite season is spring which is nature’s wake up call. I love to sit out on our deck and listen to the birds singing. Sometimes I see bunnies frolicking together in our back yard as I feel the gentle breeze blowing in my hair. The flowers are blooming as they delight in sunny days and cool evenings. Summer is okay............. however the humidity feels like a sauna and if we don’t have enough rainfall it will cause us to experience a draught! Many people love to come to the mountains in the fall to experience the leaves decked out in an array of colors.

However, I know that winter will soon arrive and will cause me to hibernate since I do not enjoy cold weather. Winter seems like such a dark season...........the birds have gone in search of sunshine, animals have hibernated, flowers are no longer blooming, and the leaves have fallen off the trees! But..............all of a sudden one morning we wake up to experience a beautiful wonderland of snow that covers everything like a blanket! Yes! There is beauty in the midst of darkness!

We experience many seasons in this life. We love the season in which everything seems to fit together. Our prayers are being answered and our faith is soaring high! But what about the season with difficult trials that tries to steal our peace and joy? This is the season in our life where we find how strong our faith really is!

But without faith it is impossible to please Him, for he that comes to God must believe that He is and that He is a rewarder of those that diligently seek Him! (Hebrews 11:6 NKJ)

The rocks remind us of hard, rough and uncomfortable places in our lives that sometimes cause us to toil arduously until we relinquish our control to God! As long as we carry the burdens everything we attempt to accomplish involves great labor and causes our problems to surmount. When we give those hardened areas of our hearts to God He becomes our firm support and source of strength. Now we no longer see the rock as a hard place but God becomes our rock!

They all ate the same spiritual food and drank the same spiritual drink; for they drank from the spiritual rock that accompanied them, and that rock was Christ. (I Corinthians 10:3-4 NIV)

The palm tree reminds us of the desert experience the Israelites endured. They came out of a season of hard labor and now were entering a season of trusting God for all their provisions. Even though they saw His hand of provision daily they still grumbled and complained in the midst of God's goodness! God's desire for them was to develop a deeper trust in Him and to grow spiritually and flourish as the palm tree does in dry seasons. Instead of receiving His promises they focused on their problems which caused them to lose hope. God wanted them to take hold of His promise of deliverance and experience the victory in their lives. Palm branches were spread out on the streets to usher Jesus in His triumphant entry! Not only does the palm tree flourish in dry deserted seasons but its branches were cut off, placed in the streets and stepped on by many people. Perhaps, this sounds like you. If you are in this desert season and do not give up………… you will be used to usher in Jesus presence in others!

But blessed is the man who trusts in the Lord, whose confidence is in Him. He will be like a tree planted by the water that sends out its roots by the stream. It does not fear when heat comes. Its leaves are always green. It has no worries in a year of drought and never fails to bear fruit. (Jeremiah 17:7-8 NIV)

What season are you in? Lift your hands and touch God today. He will not reject your prayers and will meet your needs. He knows the longing of your soul and will touch you with the Son shine of His love so………… you can reach out and touch others!

Foreword

I've been privileged to have known Jenny for a number of years. I have been a spiritual advisor to her, as well as a fellow servant of our Lord Jesus Christ in evangelistic ministry to the lost, the poor, and the hurting. I've watched Jenny grow in many areas of her spiritual walk with our Lord, through many storms and trials in her personal life as well as the testing of her faith in her spiritual life.

I am very proud of what God has accomplished in and through her. I can truly say that she has been shaped on the potters' wheel, tried and tested in the fiery furnace of affliction, and is ready to be a vessel to be used to the glory of our Lord and Savior Jesus Christ.

I can say without exception that anyone who reads this book will be both blessed and encouraged through the wealth of her experience of God's shaping hand in her life.

In His Service,

Rev. Bernard J. Carpenter

(Pastor) Bethel A.M.E. Church

Lewistown, PA

I first found out about PLM at a prayer meeting. Jenny and I attend the same church. She helped me in such a loving way to see how God loves me and how much He is concerned with each part of my life. At age sixty-nine God can still use me to show God's love to others! I thank God for Jenny and the women who make up Promise Land Ministries. It is exciting to see how God moves through each one, enhancing their gifts in drama, music, and testimonies and helping hurting men and women to feel God's love. I feel so honored to be a part of this ministry! ~ Carole Gibboney

It has been a wonderful experience sharing my love for Jesus and talking and praying with women from across the state. Living more than two hours west of Belleville makes it impossible for me to attend all the ministry meetings with prayers, planning sessions and Bible studies. but I attend when I can. In the past seven years I have experienced marital separation which led to divorce and also had breast cancer, going through chemo and radiation. It is amazing how tender my heart has become after experiencing these two major events in my life. I feel I am better able to understand the hurt and disappointments other women are going through because of my own experiences. Fred and Jenny and the PLM team have given me a lot of prayer support and in turn I want to be used by God to help women who are going through similar situations! ~ *Regina Jack*

The past few years of my life have been the toughest that I have been through. God has been strengthening my faith muscle, as Jenny calls it. What is faith? It is the confident assurance that what we hope for is going to happen. It is the evidence of things we cannot yet see. (Hebrews 11:6) As a member of the Promise Land Ministries team, I have so much support, advice and prayer. I have learned that even though what we want may not be the best thing for us or others......... God loves us and is in control even in the darkest times of our lives. When I look through the eyes of faith, I see God and all the blessings to come *~Betsy Casner*

When I came to Belleville in Nov. 2000, I was in the middle of a divorce. I had no job, no church and although I had an extended family full of people I loved very much, I did not have a close friend. God being the faithful and loving God that He is met every need including sending me a close and blessed friend in Jenny. She was leading a Bible Study in her home and invited me to attend. I saw the anointing of God on her for teaching others. Within a year, God was beginning to birth PLM. I feel so blessed and privileged to have been here from its inception and to see where it is today. One of the most amazing blessings from the Lord has been watching transformations in all of us and in others at the ministry functions. Every Tuesday evening we meet at Fred and Jenny's home for prayer, preparation, instruction and ministry. Their home is a safe haven and we are all one big family coming together to bear our souls, lay our burdens down and know that God is in our midst. There is no judging..........only love and acceptance. We allow the Holy Spirit to lead and follow His instructions in all aspects of the ministry. *~Philan Simeti*

I have gone through my own personal struggles that lead me to attend a renewal. The main struggle, which I might add that God has healed and delivered me, has been the fight with bipolar and other mental disorders. We meet a lot of women that have depression and anxiety so I can relate to other people very well that are struggling with these issues! ~ Jody Esh

I attended a women's renewal in 2006 that PLM had in our church in Lewistown. I felt there was something different about this ministry. I was dealing with a lot of guilt and pain from my daughter's drug addiction and even though by now she was on her way to becoming a mother, I still couldn't get past the questions of why didn't I see it coming and why didn't I do more to prevent it! I talked with Jenny after the renewal. She told me that I was carrying a burden of guilt! There is therefore no condemnation to them which are in Christ Jesus, who walk not after the flesh, but after the Spirit. (Romans 8:1 KJV) Jenny showed me how satan had a hold on me and how through the power and authority in Jesus Name I was able to lay it at Jesus' feet and move on! I became part of the ministry team in October 2008 and hope to be an encouragement to other mothers that are going through addictions with their children. My daughter now has two children and owns her home. There is hope and power in praying in Jesus Name. ~ *Maria Stringfellow*

I came to an open prayer meeting at Fred and Jenny's home. I met the team of PLM and my life has not been the same since and never will again. I have been a Christian for as long as I can remember. But it was on that day I met God face to face for the first time in my life. I felt and understood the reality of Him and His love and I accepted His love. I willingly received from Him the love that He had for so long desired to give me. Through the presence of the Holy Spirit, the faith of the women and the prayers that evening, for the first time in my life I witnessed that God was as real as you and me and that personal and intimate relationships between man and God do exist. He wants nothing more than to have a personal relationship with every one of us. He's not just a character in a story. He is real! His heart breaks for each and every one of you. Won't you open your hearts to Him and feel His love? ~ *Amy Freed*

I have wanted to serve the Lord for a long time. I always felt as though I had to be perfect to serve Him and I knew I was never even close. Being a part of PLM has shown me that God uses our imperfections and problems to help others and their walk with the Lord. I know now that I do not have to be perfect to serve our Lord. If we were perfect and did not have problems...would we really need him? I am thankful that we have a God who loves us just the way we are and He uses us and all of our imperfections to mold us to be more like Jesus. He takes our problems and fills us with hope, joy and peace!!! Psalms 136:1 Oh, give thanks to the Lord, for He is good; His loving kindness continues forever! ~ *Beth White*

PLM is a God-centered ministry! We include him in the entire decision making and bathe everything in prayer. The added benefit of this ministry has been how it has helped me to grow emotionally and spiritually. I keep connected to a group of women who encourage me to come up higher in my relationship with God and to let go of everything that hinders that walk. I have been through a lot of deep pain and grief in my life. I have experienced a lot of loss. I have also walked through many dark years of infertility. Through some close relationships and of course my walk with God, I have been in the process of healing. God has been faithful to me day by day. I want to be available to be an encouragement to others who are struggling with losses of their own. ~ *Chris Prough*

I learned about PLM during a mother/daughter banquet at our church that Jenny was the speaker. My son was diagnosed with a malignant brain tumor months prior to meeting her. In the months following our son's illness, Jenny was a prayer support during this sadness in our life. Throughout our son's short life on earth (three years old) God answered two prayers that I had prayed before Zeb became ill. I was able to spend more time with Zeb (since I worked full-time) and I became closer to God. God answered my prayers, perhaps not in the way I would have liked, but according to His will for my life! I will never be able to thank Him enough for getting me through every day without my baby! I simply want to share my many amazing God-filled experiences with everyone who wishes to hear them in hopes to bring more of His children back to Him! ~ Amy Franklin

I was so taken by God's complete control of His entire service. It is not run by people but by God through people. I had been hungry to be a part of something God was actually in charge of.

I was immediately drawn to this ministry. I now live in South Carolina, but am able to attend the meetings by speaker phone weekly. Three years ago I lost my best friend and sister to a tragic death. She had two teenage girls at the time with many teenage struggles. My husband and I took the girls in as our own, along with our own two teenage daughters with all their struggles. Needless to say, it was the hardest year and a half that I ever went through. I sat at the Lord's feet daily just to make it through another day. Many times I lay at his feet weeping! God answered my prayer when I asked Him to please use every hardship I have to minister and bring comfort to many others! ~ *Lisa Salyards*

Preface

"It's time to heal the church to heal the world." This is the message that God has implanted in my heart. There is always a light at the end of the tunnel. But.........how do you get to the end when darkness is all around?

The Lord gave me this vision. I saw Jesus with a huge foot in the air that actually looked like He was wearing a large boot. Then He spoke these words to me, "It's time to boot the enemy out of my church then I will take my position that I intended for my creation."

My message to my church is not an easy one. But.....Oh, how freeing it is when my church listens to my truth and allows me to change their hearts. My message is hope in this hopeless world! My children who heed my words are where I will build my church. I am looking for a new church full of my love that will penetrate the darkness of hearts. I am rising up my army in these last days that will not fight among themselves but will know how to battle the enemy. My love will conquer anything that tries to come against my children. I am preparing the way of love to my church. My children must have me as their foundation or they will crumble and fall away from me. I am the truth which brings life and leads the way in this world of waywardness!

Then He gave me another vision: I saw a church building with Jesus standing beside it. Jesus had something in His hand and was chipping away at the building. Then He said, "I am chipping away at the ways of the world in my church. When my love reigns in my church they will penetrate the world. I am calling my church to reign over the world not the world to reign over my church!"

When soldiers enlist in the armed forces they have to go through Boot Camp first! Why? So they can gain strength, knowledge, boldness and courage when they face the enemy. They must face their enemies within before they can face the enemy in war. In the face of fear they must have boldness and courage. They must also learn how to be a team together and walk in unity and be willing to die for not only their country but for their fellow man. They must know how to face adversity……weather conditions, cold and heat and storms etc. They must face the loneliness of not having their friends and family with them and keep the faith that they will remain alive and come back to their loved ones. They must be disciplined to rise up early and exercise to keep their bodies healthy and strong. Sometimes they must go for days with nothing to eat. They must learn to respect authority and not take offense from others. And…………they must know their weapons and how to use them and where to use them! Most of all they need to know their Commander-in-Chief!

Do you know Him? The Apostle Paul introduced Him as, "The God Who produced and formed the world and all things in it, being Lord of heaven and earth, does not dwell in handmade shrines. Neither is He served by human hands, as though He lacked anything for it is He himself who gives life and breath and all things to all people. And He made from one (common origin, one source, one blood) all nations of men to settle on the face of the earth, having definitely determined (their) allotted periods of time and the fixed boundaries of their habitation (their settlements, lands, and abodes), So that they should seek God, in the hope that they might feel after Him and find Him, although He is not far from each one of us. For in Him we live and move and have our being; as even some of your (own) poets have said, for we are also His offspring." (Acts 17:24-28 AMP)

The Greek meaning of feel is touch. Have you reached out and touched God?

I invite you to walk through the pages of my journey of brokenness that led me to encounter and fall in love with my Commander-in-Chief. Therefore I willingly enlisted in God's Boot Camp that brought me to experience His Camp Hope!

Acknowledgments

January 19, 2003, I was given a stunning dream by the Holy Spirit. I saw many people surrounding each other with great excitement! I saw someone holding a book. In my dream I had a desire to see what they were reading. Suddenly, someone turned the book around for me to see the title! The title was "Touch Me" by Jenny Hagemeyer!

At 4:00 in the morning I woke up and began to write under the inspiration of the Holy Spirit! Now you need to understand that I do not and can not write without His inspiration.

What an honor and privilege it is to be used as God's vessel to bring healing to His children!

Thank you Father, Jesus and Holy Spirit for showing me how to touch your heart and in turn inspire others to touch you daily!

Thank you, my husband, Fred for your love and commitment to God and to our marriage in the hard times as well as the good ones. You are my gift from God!

Thank you, Mom for all your encouragement in writing this book and allowing me to share our family with others so they too can be touched by God.

Thank you, Regina for your friendship and the many hours you spent looking over each page for editing.

Thank you, Rev. Carpenter for always giving us encouragement to press on with the ministry.

Thank you, Promise Land Ministries team sisters for your love and devotion to our God and to all of us.

Thank you, Pastor Steve and Michelle for all your love and prayers.

How blessed I am to have all of you!

Introduction

The meal was nearly over at a church mother/daughter banquet. I had written a message and was prepared with all my notes that were bathed in prayer.

Five minutes before I stood up to speak, the Lord gave me a vision. I saw myself holding a pan filled with a fine powder that looked like gold dust. However, as I began to scrutinize the pan very carefully while gently shaking it, I found many gold nuggets buried underneath the dust that were solid and had weight to them. At that moment God told me that He was changing the message.

I was in my second year of ministry that began in 2002! This had never happened to me before. However, I felt a deep peace even though I had no idea what I would share. I had given the Holy Spirit complete control of my mouth and knew that when I opened my mouth God would fill it!

As God used me as His vessel, the word of the Lord began to touch us with His truth and the oil of His love poured into those dark, dry and dusty places within our hearts. As I spoke,

His nuggets took root in our spirits and caused our faith to rise higher than we had ever experienced. I began to tell them about the vision and how God wanted us to mine for His gold. I talked with them about shaking off the dust of negativity and allowing the Holy Spirit to speak His nuggets that would bring healing to their souls!

Shake off your dust, rise up, sit enthroned, O Jerusalem. Free yourself from the chains on your neck O captive Daughter of Zion. (Isaiah 52:2 NIV)

Throughout this book you will find many gold nuggets from the Holy Spirit to meditate on that will bring inspiration that have been received through visions, dreams and God's spoken and written word. By no means do I believe that all dreams are prophetic. Dreams can be fragments of our imaginations or demonic. Dreams may also be inspired by the Holy Spirit to bring about truth and lead us onto His path. I do believe that God desires fellowship with us daily and chooses how to speak to us when our hearts are open to hear from Him! We need to seek God for His divine wisdom, discernment and revelations. Just as you have a camera in your mind that continually rewinds painful pictures of the past............a vision is an image that is imprinted on your mind through the Holy Spirit that brings understanding in the midst of chaos and confusion in your life. God is calling us to be filled with His Holy Spirit to walk, talk and hear in the spirit.

Our vision is limited as we look through the eye of a microscope. God sees everything through His spiritual telescope! When we receive a vision the Holy Spirit places His super vision with our natural eyesight which brings His supernatural revelations!

So, I am asking you to shake off the dust of negativity in your mind before you continue. Lean not to your own understanding and allow God to lead you onto His path. Through the Holy

Spirit's leading our prayer is that you will be enlightened in your mind, refreshed in your soul, and energized in your spirit as your journey leads you to an abundant life filled with God's blessings!

God bless you,

Jenny

Touch Me

I have exciting news for you today! Are you ready? Here goes.........God wants to change you!

Most of you know the song Celebration! Well, this is what God wants us to do. When I announced this in one of our renewals, we actually played the Celebration song!

I can hear you saying, "You said it was exciting!"

Think of this! Our awesome, loving heavenly Father desires time with you. He has so much for us that we can't even think or imagine!

You are God's child! You are loved by God! You are a new creation! You are created in His image! You are called by God! You are the apple of His eye! You have the mind of Christ! You are God's workmanship! Wow! Can you imagine that? When the enemy comes to tell you that you aren't worthy, speak His words over yourself! It's not about you. It's about Him!

One day I was on my treadmill thinking all kinds of negative thoughts about myself! The Lord spoke in my heart, "Jenny, this is not about you..........this is about me!" He began to tell me that He created me for His plan, not mine. When God was placing on my heart to start Promise Land Ministries, there were people that didn't understand the timing. I kept waiting and was in fear of what others thought and said.

Then one day, God gave me a vision. He showed me a wide open door with Him standing there waiting to usher me out. I was standing there biting my nails in fear of making the wrong moves.

"Job replied to the Lord, "I know that you can do all things; no plan of yours can be thwarted." (Job 42:2 NIV)

I began to realize that no matter what happens in my life nothing can succeed against the Lord. Actually, I received a revelation of this that began to change my life!

Jeremiah 17:9-10 says, "The heart is deceitful above all things, and it is exceedingly perverse and corrupt and severely mortally sick! Who can know it (perceive, understand, be acquainted with his own heart and mind? Who can understand it?" (AMP)

God understands everything that is going on in our heart. He knows when there is deep rooted pain that we aren't even aware of and what causes us to react in anger, selfishness, fear, or pride instead of responding in love, peace and joy. He has watched all of the rejections that we have suffered in life. He sees the darkness in our hearts. The good news is nothing can ever separate us from His love.

"I'm absolutely convinced that nothing—nothing living or dead, angelic or demonic, today or tomorrow, high or low, thinkable or unthinkable—absolutely nothing can get between us and God's love because of the way that Jesus our Master has embraced us." (Romans 8:38-39 Message)

I remember when my brother was a little boy receiving a spanking from my mother. She told him that she spanked him because she loved him. One day after his normal spanking, he turned to her and said," I wish you wouldn't love me so much!" Knowing who we are and how much God loves us should make us want to throw a party in God's honor! This is why we celebrate CHANGE! C'mon, break out your praises to God and let's have church!

I can hear some of you saying, "I don't need to change! After all I've been praying for my spouse, children, church, friends and my circumstances to change! If only they would change, I would be happy!"

Most of us do not look at change as exciting! We're used to the same old same olds! Same old arguments that never get resolved, same old weight that never comes off year after year, same old boring jobs, same old tiredness and feelings of discouragement, same old smiles on our faces for other people not to see the real me inside. After all, if they knew the real me, they wouldn't want to associate with me! How about the same old thoughts that keep reoccurring such as we're not pretty enough, smart enough, or good enough!

What about the same old gossip that we join in since we only tell it to others so they can pray? How about the same old marriages that have lost communication and excitement? What about the same old church services and believe it or not, the same old pews that we sit in Sunday after Sunday and would be very upset if someone else would take our seat? C'mon, let's be honest! What about the same old jealousy of others that their gift is greater than ours?

So, how can we live with the same old same olds and see our circumstances, spouses, family, and friends from God's perspective?

The definition of perspective is the relative importance of facts or matters from any special point of view, judgment of facts, circumstances, etc. with regard to their importance. (Funk and Wagnall)

In other words, what is God's point of view in all of these people and situations?

One of the girls on our team had flown to Philadelphia. She was telling me that when she looked down...............she was amazed at seeing a whole city at once! This is what God sees!

He sees the whole journey of our lives from the beginning to the end.

"Let us fix our eyes on Jesus, the author and perfector (finisher of our faith, who for the joy set before him endured the cross, scorning its shame, and sat down at the right hand of the throne of God!" (Hebrews 12:2 NIV)

"Remember this, fix it in mind, take it to heart, you rebels, Remember the former things, those of long ago, I am God, and there is no other, I am God, and there is none like me. I make known the end from the beginning from ancient times, what is still to come. I say, my purpose will stand, and I will do all that I please." (Isaiah 46:8-10 NIV)

"It is done; I am the Alpha and Omega, the Beginning and the End. To Him who is thirsty I will give to drink without cost from the spring of the water of life. He who overcomes will inherit all this, and I will be his God and he will be my son."(Revelations 21:6 NIV)

The longer I walk with God, the more I can see what He has done in my life in allowing the good and the bad.

"I form the light and create darkness. I bring prosperity and create disaster. I, the Lord, do all these things." (Isaiah 45:7 NIV)

When you go through the valley of difficulties, God is planting seeds of opportunities that will come out of the adversity in your life.

Adversity is God's opportunity to accomplish perseverance, endurance and strength which produces growth within you. As rain falls on a garden and brings growth to the plants, His Holy Spirit reigns on your heart to produce growth in your spirit. Many of you have wounded spirits. Satan's goal is to crush your spirit and harden your heart. God's purpose is to soften your heart and bring life into the deadness of your spirit. When your heart is hardened the enemy speaks his poison into your mind. If your mind is not renewed with God's word, those evil thoughts lead to action.

"And do not be conformed to this world but be transformed by the renewing of your mind that you may prove what is that good and acceptable and perfect will of God." (Romans 12:2 NKJ)

When the mind is being renewed with God's word a battle of spirit and flesh begins. As your heart is softened and more darkness is removed, more walls come down and the spirit comes to life and connects with God's spirit. We then begin to recognize the power within us to overcome the enemy in our heart and mind.

I believe that we need to get a bigger picture of who God is! If we would truly grasp the largeness of our God, we wouldn't fret over anything!

One day as I was meditating on the Lord, He gave me a vision of Jesus holding part of the cross with His arms slumped over it. He said, "When you doubt my love for you, you place me on part of the cross. I didn't die so you could live part way. I died so you could live fully through my resurrection power!"

"The thief comes only in order to steal and kill and destroy. I came that they may have and enjoy life, and have an abundance (to the full, till it overflows." (John 10:10 AMP)

The word *abundantly* is from the Greek word *periossos*, and it means to be above, beyond what is regular, extraordinary, or even exceeding. (Strongs)

The definition of exceeding is plentiful supply; abounding. (Funk and Wagnall)

The life Jesus offers is richly loaded with vitality for us to continually possess and way beyond whatever we could think or imagine.

I am reminded of a volcano. When it erupts there is no stopping it. When you asked Jesus into your heart you received His eruptive power within your spirit that overflows to others since it cannot be contained! God doesn't want us to be satisfied with a mediocre life. I believe that God has called us to an

Extraordinary! Exciting! Invigorating! Encouraging! Inspirational! Rejuvenating! Uplifting life!

So if we live with the same olds day after day, how do we have a life of plentiful supply of love, joy, peace, patience, goodness, meekness, gentleness and self control?

As I was preparing this message for one of our renewals, the Lord spoke in my heart an acronym for each letter of abundant!

A Bold, Undefeated, New, Daring, Abnormal, Nonresistant, Tapestry!

I was so excited and realized that this is what an abundant life is all about! As you read the following pages, meditate on each word and consider where this fits in your life! Ask yourself these questions. Am I living an abundant life or is my life full of discouragement? Do I see myself as a victim of my past and my surrounding circumstances or am I aware of the victory in laying down all of my burdens for God to have the opportunity to show Himself strong? Do I really want to change?

If you are ready, let's move on to have an encounter with God and receive an avalanche of His blessings!

Bold

The Greek word for **bold** is *parresia* which gives the idea of boldness, frankness, forthrightness, and outspokenness. (Strongs)

"For we have not a high priest which cannot be touched with the feelings of our infirmities, but was in all points tempted like as we are, yet without sin. Let us therefore come boldly to the throne of grace that we may obtain mercy, and find grace to help in time of need." (Hebrews 4:15-16 KJ)

God wants us to come boldly to Him daily with frankness!

One day as I was praying, I heard God say, " Don't give me that spiritual jargon.............I want you to be gut honest with me!" When I began to tell it like it really was...... .....I heard Him say, "Now...... I can work!"

As we go on this journey of life, many of us don't have a clue of God's plan for us. We're just ordinary men and women with ordinary jobs getting through ordinary days. But...Jeremiah 29:11 talks about God having plans for us, plans to bring hope and a future and not to harm us. (AMP) He knows what He is doing. He has it all planned out and has written His own story for us. He will take care of us and never abandon us.

When we call on Him.............He will listen and answer us! When we look for Him, we will find Him!

Let's talk about two people who went looking for Jesus. The first one, a man named Jairus, a ruler of the synagogue whose daughter was dying and the second, a woman who was bleeding for twelve years!

The story begins in Luke 8:40. "Now when Jesus returned, a crowd welcomed Him for they were all expecting Him." The Amplified Bible says, "They were all waiting and looking for Him." Notice the crowd not only was looking and waiting for Him but they were expecting Jesus to come. That tells me that they weren't just taking glances with little hope that He might show up. First of all they had heard He was coming. They believed what they had heard. So they waited with great expectation for His arrival.

Can you imagine the excitement? Perhaps they had heard how Jesus had removed the legion of demons from the man who had been bound in chains and tortured for many years. Had they heard the man's cries of torment and watched him break his chains and be driven into tombs? Did they tell each other to stay away from that crazy man that lives like an animal? Did they fear every time they heard rumors that he was loose and might come to their homes since Gadarenes was about five miles southeast of the Sea of Galilee? This crazy man was delivered instantly of the pain and torment of his past and was giving his testimony!

I am reminded of a song that I sang as a child......"This little light of mine. I'm going to let it shine."

This man was living in tombs not in a house like everyone else. Now he was made free by Jesus and commissioned to go tell others!

The word tomb is taken from a Greek word *mnemeion* that means grave or sepulcher. (Strongs)

Satan thought this man was dead spiritually, physically and emotionally! But……Jesus freed him from the bondage of so many years. How many of you feel that you have been pronounced dead by the enemy and don't feel or see the light of Jesus in your life? Call out to Jesus now and He will come and shine His light on those dark areas in your heart and mind. Jesus is the answer for all of your problems. He is standing at the door of your heart waiting for you to open up to Him. Won't you reach out and take His hand today? He will remove the shame and guilt of your past mistakes! Place all of your burdens at His feet and He will replace those burdens with His peace, love and joy for you. He is here to make you free today!

"Therefore if the Son makes you free you shall be free indeed!" (John 8:36 NKJ)

Jesus told him to return to his own house and tell others the great things God had done for him. He was no longer living in darkness but now had the light of Jesus shining on him. Now he was called to bring that light to his community! What is God calling you to do?

Come with me as we envision the thoughts of this crowd. Could this man Jesus heal them of their illnesses too? Can you feel the great anticipation among them? Who was in this crowd? Can you picture the lame, blind, possessed and people stricken with diseases that were beyond all cures? Would their sight be restored for them to finally see their family, friends and God's creative hand? Would they be able to throw away their crutches and walk? Would they no longer be shunned and rejected by others because of their disease? Would Jesus be a respecter of persons and only heal children and those of importance?

Jesus began to walk through the crowd. Can you imagine their thoughts? Maybe this is my last chance to receive healing. Will I blow it if I wait? Will He come to me or should I break through the crowd and go to Him? Will I miss Him passing by? Will He notice me?

Suddenly a man decides to go to Jesus without waiting.

"And there came a man named Jairus, who had (for a long time) been a director of the synagogue; and falling at the feet of Jesus, he begged Him to come to his house."
(Luke 8:41 AMP)

Notice Jairus fell at His feet. He didn't tap Him on the shoulder or ask Him to come. He was a desperate man that had a twelve year old daughter whom he loved very much. He was a broken father that was pleading for his beloved daughter's life at Jesus feet!

"My sacrifice (the sacrifice acceptable) to God is a broken spirit; a broken and contrite heart (broken down with sorrow for sin and humbly and thoroughly penitent) such, O God, You will not despise."
(Psalm 51:17AMP)

Without a word to Jairus, Jesus begins to make His way through the crowd walking with Jairus and His disciples. People are pressing against Jesus so much that He is almost crushed. Suddenly, a woman that has been bleeding for twelve years without any cure for healing touches the edge of His cloak and immediately her bleeding stops.

Now, wait a minute! Wasn't Jesus on His way with the disciples to Jairus' home to pray for his daughter? I wonder what was going through Jairus' mind.

Was he upset that someone caused Jesus to stop and not continue moving forward to his house? Surely, Jesus knew this was very urgent! After all, his daughter was dying! Wasn't his answer to prayer more important than hers?

Has this ever happened to you? You were moving right along with Jesus and all of a sudden your life came to a standstill. You were praying and praying yet nothing was happening? Was God saying no or wait? I believe that God always answers prayer. He says yes, no or wait!

"Be still and know that I am God. I will be exalted among the nations. I will be exalted in the earth!" (Psalm 46:10 NIV)

In Galatians 5:22 one of the fruits of the spirit is patience. You know, one of those times when you pray for patience but want it right now. One day the Lord spoke in my heart that patience is the key that unlocks the door to His heart! But...................... we don't want to wait! In this microwave world where everything is at our fingertips quickly we don't like waiting.

But...........what is Jesus doing? Jesus asked a question, "Who touched me?" All of a sudden the noise of the crowd comes to a hush and an awe of His presence. Fear begins to grip them. They can feel lumps in their throats, as everyone denies touching Jesus. The disciples break the silence. "Master, the people are crowding and pressing against you." It seems like a no brainier question except that Jesus says, "I know someone has touched me for the power has gone out from me." (Luke 8:46 NIV)

What kind of a touch is this? This is a special touch! This woman has been waiting with great expectation in this crowd. Has she been crying out to God for many years for this healing? Was this how God would answer her prayer through Jesus? Was it her time to be healed? Perhaps she has waited for days, weeks or months after she heard about Jesus who has been going from town to town touching and healing. Would He come to her or should she be so bold as to touch Him? Would she have the courage to touch Him or would she cower in fear? What if she touched Him and she remained unchanged? Would she feel less important? Would she dare to risk being rejected? Would she be arrested for touching a Jewish man since she was unclean? Was she trying to remember if she had heard anyone say they had touched His clothing? No, all she had heard was how Jesus touched them. Now the day had finally come. She has touched the hem of His garment and she is healed. Jesus is waiting for an answer to who touched Him. Should she tell Him? Would she lose her healing? She must step forward and throw off all of these negative thoughts! She must focus on Jesus and not the fear! It's time to humble herself in front of this multitude of people! She falls at Jesus feet trembling as she begins to tell why she touched Him.

Jesus says, "Daughter, your faith (your confidence and trust in me) has made you well. Go (enter into peace, untroubled, undisturbed well-being)."
(Luke 8:48 AMP)

Did you hear that? He called her daughter! If she didn't know who she was before that day..............today she knew that she was His daughter!

I remember when God gave me a revelation of being his daughter! I had been telling the Lord that it was so hard for me to see myself as His daughter. I was going through a really tough situation and God said, "I have called you into this realm to teach you who you really are. Unless you know who you are, you won't know who I am. Listen to that inner voice inside of you. Hear what I am saying. Do not listen to the words of the enemy. You are my daughter! I want you to ponder on that and see the reality of this!"

The Hebrew word for daughter is *bath* which means apple of my eye. (Strongs)

"Rejoice greatly O daughter (apple of my eye) of Zion. Shout, Daughter of Jerusalem. See your King comes to you." (Zechariah 9:9 AMP)

He began to show me how important my daughter was to me and how much I loved her no matter what!

When my daughter was a new born she would cry all hours of the night. We never forget those sleepless nights! However, it didn't matter because when I would hear that cry, I would come to her rescue. I would pick her up and hold her close to my breast and feed her.

"The righteous cry out and the Lord hears them; He delivers them from all their troubles." (Psalm 34:17 NIV)

When she became a toddler and was playing outside, sometimes she would fall down and skin her knee. I would hear that terrible shriek and come running. She would point to her boo boo and ask me to fix it. So, I would carry her into the house, put peroxide on it to counteract any infection, blow on it and then put a band aid on so it was protected. That would satisfy her and she would go out and play again.

"God is our refuge and strength, a very present help in trouble." (Psalm 46:1 NIV)

There were times when she would have a dream that would scare her and wake her up and again I heard, "Mommy!" I would come to her bedside and tell her everything is okay and she would be comforted by my words. After awhile, she would drift back to sleep.

"You shall not be afraid of the terror by night or of the arrows that flies by day." (Psalm 91:5 NKJ))

When she was sick, she would cry, "Mommy, my belly hurts!" I would set a basin in case she would have to throw up, give her medicine and try to make her as comfortable as I could. Then I would sit by her bed until she drifted back to sleep.

"As a mother comforts her child, so will I comfort you and you will be comforted over Jerusalem." (Isaiah 66:13 NIV)

When she was too little to turn on the light, I would flip on the switch so she would not have to be afraid of the dark.

"You are my lamp, O Lord. The Lord turns my darkness into light."
(II Samuel 22:29 NIV)

When she would go shopping with me, I would hold her hand so she didn't get lost.

"If I rise on the wings of the dawn, I will settle on the far side of the sea. Even there your hand will guide me. Your right hand will hold me fast."
(Psalm 139:10 NIV)

Jesus not only called the woman daughter but He saw the faith and confidence that she had in knowing that He was her Jehovah Rophe, healer. It took great boldness to let others know of her bleeding since in those days it was considered to be unclean. Jesus was pleased with her faith, confidence and trust in Him and told her to go in peace.

But.........just as He was speaking to the woman, someone came from Jairus' house and announced that his daughter had died and he was not to trouble the teacher anymore. What was going on in Jairus mind? Did he feel resentment for the woman in delaying Jesus? Was he angry at Jesus for stopping? There is no record in the Bible of what he said, only what Jesus said. Can you put yourself in Jairus' place? Jesus was walking with him towards his house before his daughter died. All of a sudden this woman came out of the crowd and touched Jesus. Not only has the power gone out of Jesus but now his daughter is dead.

This woman received her healing that delayed his daughter from being healed. What kind of a man is this Jesus who heals others and lets a little child die?

We've all heard that God comes in the eleventh hour to test our faith, but sometimes He comes after midnight! When Jesus heard that the daughter had died, He said, "Do not be afraid, only believe, and she will be made well." (Luke 8:50 KJ)

Okay, there you have it! Jesus said it and now it was up to Jairus to believe it! I am reminded of a song that says, "God said it and I believe it. That settles it for me!"

Jesus tells the little girl to arise. Her spirit returned and she arose immediately! God honored the faith of both Jairus and the woman but chose to answer each of them in different ways and in His timing!

"For my thoughts are not your thoughts, neither are your ways my ways, says the Lord. For as the heavens are higher than the earth, so are my ways higher than your ways and my thoughts than your thoughts." (Isaiah 55:8-9 NIV)

Perhaps you are wondering where God is in your situation right now. Do you or someone close to you need to get Jesus' attention? Are you touching the hem of Jesus' garment? Are you feeling discouraged and feel that God has forgotten you? May I be so bold as to tell you to run to Jesus? He is here to sweep you into His arms and hold you as His little child. Just as your children run to you for comfort, He wants to comfort you. Some of you are saying, "But I don't know Him that way? I've never heard him speak to me."

For many years, God was a Bible God to me. I accepted Jesus into my heart when I was six years old in a Christian & Missionary Alliance church however; I never knew that I could have a personal relationship with Him. I was eighteen years old when I married the first time. Because we were so young, my husband was my whole world. We went to church every Sunday. In 1981 I had fifteen planters warts removed from my feet in the hospital and woke up with a back injury. No one seemed to know what happened to me. I suffered so much that I could not turn my head from side to side. I could only look straight ahead. Finally, I was diagnosed with a ruptured disk. The doctor scheduled a test in the hospital, but I told him that I wanted to wait. I was a displayer for a decorating company and had a plan to sell a certain amount of accessories to win a trip to meet with the president of the company. Another lady traveled with me to help set up the displays and carry my pictures and other accessories. Eventually, we became best friends and still continue that close relationship. By the end of the year, the pain had intensified and I had to stop the interior shows three weeks before the contest ended. I was $2,500 from the goal set by the company. I was so close, yet so far away from being one of the winners!

Maybe you feel that way with Jesus. Some days we feel so close to Him and other days we are asking, "Where are you?"

One day I was praying and felt the Lord laying two people on my heart that I needed to forgive. I knew that I needed to approach them before I went into the hospital. One of the ladies had gossiped about me and had really wounded me. I had chosen to ignore her and not confront it. I knew that God was asking me to talk with her. Neither one of the two responded the way I would have liked. The one denied ever saying anything nasty about me and pretended to be my friend. The other one was very nonchalant and did not take me seriously. However, I knew that I had been obedient to the Lord and wasn't responsible for their response!

The doctor scheduled a test two weeks before Christmas in the hospital. After the test, a man walked into my room wearing a white coat. I assumed he was an intern or a doctor, but I didn't recognize him. He took my hand and asked me, "If you would die tonight, where would you go?" I thought that was a strange question but I said, "I would go to heaven to be with Jesus." He smiled and walked out of the room. I never saw him again. I asked about him and no one had seen him. I believe that I was visited by an angel. Afterwards, the doctor decided that I was too young to have back surgery and cancelled the surgery. I was released from the hospital with continuous chronic pain in my body. The doctor placed me in traction but the pain was not alleviated.

I began to have recurrent nightmares of waking up paralyzed, and had many sleepless and restless nights. Sometimes the nightmares were unbearable and I would waken with terror in my heart and my body quaking.

Finally, I became desperate and cried out to God. I sat at my dining room table and said. "I don't care if you ever heal me; I will serve you no matter what, even if I am in a wheelchair." I felt a tremendous release in my spirit even though the pain remained in my physical body. I knew that God was about to do something profound in my life!

In Feb 1982 my best friend invited me to a women's Aglow meeting. Some ladies laid hands on me and prayed. Immediately the pain of so many months was finally gone and I received the Baptism of the Holy Spirit. In a vision I saw Jesus with something sparkling in His hand. I didn't understand what I had seen but knew that God would reveal this in His timing.

At the end of that year, I felt the Lord speaking into my heart that I was about to experience major changes in my life.

"Not everyone who says to me, 'Lord, Lord,' will enter the kingdom of heaven, but only he who does the will of my Father who is in heaven. Many will say to me on that day, 'Lord, Lord,' did we not prophesy in your name and in your name drive out demons and perform many miracles? Then I will tell them plainly, I never knew you, away from me, you evildoers!" (Matthew 7: 21-23 NIV)

He began to show me that I needed to get my spiritual house in order! I was going to church three times a week but barely reading my Bible. I knew Him as a Bible God but not my personal Savior! One day I was reading my Bible and became so frustrated. I took my Bible in my hand and held it up to God. I said, "I'm sorry, but I don't understand it and to be honest, I don't even like reading the Bible! However, I am going to believe that you are my teacher and when I open your word, you will begin to teach me." I began to wonder if God would be angry with me. I had always pictured Him like a strict demanding drill sergeant enforcing His commands while keeping a record of my sins. At that moment I stood still and waited. Suddenly I felt His presence flood my soul. As I basked in His love, I could hear Him say, "I want you to know me." From that moment on the Bible came alive to me. I opened up His word and my spirit received it like a sponge. I could feel my dry parched spirit soaking in His living water!

"He who believes in Me (who cleaves to and trusts in and relies on Me) as the Scripture has said, From his innermost being shall flow (continuously) springs and rivers of living water." (John 7:38 AMP)

In January 1983, we discovered that our son had severe scoliosis. On June 3, 1983, our daughter's twelfth birthday, my husband of fifteen years called me on the phone and said he was leaving. Our dog was put to sleep in July and in October my uncle, whom I loved very much, died suddenly!

One day I was asking God for encouragement. I opened my Bible to Habakkuk 3:11 that says, "Sun and the moon stood still in the heavens at the glint of your flying arrows, at the lightning of your flashing spear." (NIV)

Some interpretations say glistening or glittering spear.

God revealed to me what I had seen in my first vision that was sparkling in Jesus hand when I received the Baptism of the Holy Spirit at the Aglow meeting. In this scripture God was portrayed as a Warrior with a bow, arrows and a spear!

That day I knew in my heart God would fight for me even when I couldn't fight for myself! I knew that God had a plan for me even though I couldn't see or understand how He was going to take me through this separation.

In the beginning, my reaction was shock. Then I tried to be spiritual and pretend the problem didn't exist. As days turned into weeks, my emotions began to control me. My weight dropped quickly. I felt the loneliness, jealousy, hatred, self pity and anger well up inside of me. Satan began to shoot poisonous darts into my mind. I would wake up at night and try to figure out why, how and what I did wrong. Gradually I started entertaining suicidal thoughts. I was filled with guilt and shame and had Christian friends much like Job who helped to heap guilt and condemnation on me. I feared that my life was over and would never change. I couldn't see my way through the dark cloud that hung over me. I felt the shame of going through a divorce as a Christian and saw myself as a failure. I was rejected by my husband and some friends. One woman told me they didn't have anyone in their church that was divorced. She told me they kick them out! Most of all, I felt rejected by God! Where was He? Didn't He love me anymore? Was He angry and ashamed of me too? I became weary of waking up every day. I not only was separated from my husband but even worse I felt separated from God! I began to spend less time in the word. I felt like I was trudging up a hill and could never reach the top. I had a huge tidal wave of pain and was drowning in my sorrows. Even in the sunny days I felt the eeriness and chill of the darkness in my spirit. The evil was thriving and my emotions remained in the closet of my heart.

One day my emotions came crashing in with all the pain. Even though I had two children who needed me, my focus was on ending my life. I didn't care about anything or anyone including myself. As far as I was concerned, my life was over. I had reached a dead end! It was time to end this excruciating pain! I couldn't get the thoughts out of my mind. Over and over, I heard, "You messed up your life." "You are such a failure!" "It's time to end this!" "No one cares about you and they won't miss you!" "No one loves you!" "God doesn't love you!" Satan was speaking words of death to my mind and I was too weak to resist him.

"Submit yourselves unto God. Resist the devil and he will flee from you."
(James 4:7 KJ)

I wanted out of the valley of sorrows but couldn't find my way out! I was allowing my mind to become a play ground for the devil and was losing my way! Satan had placed his bait on the rod of my mind and was reeling me in. My strength to move forward was waning.

"Listen to my prayer O God do not ignore my plea, hear me and answer me. My thoughts trouble me and I am distraught at the voice of the enemy and the stares of the wicked for they bring down suffering upon me and revile me in their anger."
(Psalm 55:1-3 NIV)

Finally, the day had come for my quick fix to end all this pain! I had played it over and over in my mind and knew exactly what I was going to do. However, God had a greater plan! One phone call brought me to my senses and saved my life! I was scheduled to see a counselor the next day. He called me and said, "Jenny, if you take your life, you are not allowing God to do with this situation what He wants to do!" Anger began to rise up from the very depths of my heart and I began to scream and cry until there were no more tears left! My Warrior had come to my rescue. He had pulled out His bow, arrows and spears against the enemy who was stealing my mind, and wanted to destroy my life! Praise God! He is faithful! He is standing here right now ready to fight for you.

Perhaps you can identify with the pain of rejection. Maybe you feel that your burden is too great. Don't allow the enemy to keep you burdened, weary, stooped low and bowed down another day longer!

There is a story about a little boy that was outside with his mother. As they were walking, he began to pick up all kinds of stones. Some stones were very heavy but he continued to place them in his bag. Soon his bag became so heavy that he could hardly carry it. As he walked back home with his mother he held on to the bag. He was so tired and worn out yet he would not give up the bag. His mother wanted to take it from him but he wouldn't let go. But all of a sudden daddy was home! The little boy was so delighted to see his daddy that he forgot about the bag and dropped it at his daddy's feet. His daddy picked him up and held him in his arms! (Author unknown)

Your Daddy is here! Run to Him and drop those burdens at His feet. He will pick you up and hold you close to Him!

Undefeated

Do you see yourself as defeated by the enemy or **undefeated** because of Jesus' death and resurrection?

The first part of John 10:10 says, "The thief (Satan comes to kill, steal and destroy)." (AMP)

In I Samuel 17: Israel is faced with their enemy the Philistine armies' champion Goliath who comes to defy Israel daily!

The word Champion was taken from a Hebrew expression that means a warrior who fights in single combat and is a go between for the entire army!
(Strongs)

Goliath's height was six cubits and a span which would be comparable to 9ft. 9 inches. Think about the tallest basketball player that you have ever heard of and add at least two more feet! While the other troops had leather helmets, Goliath had a bronze helmet and wore a coat of scale armor of bronze weighing 5,000 shekels which was approximately 125 pounds. He had bronze armor on his legs and a bronze javelin between his shoulders. In other words, the javelin was strapped to his back and was designed for hurling. The staff of his spear was like a weaver's beam (rod) his spear head weighed 600 shekels (approx. 17 pounds); and a shield bearer went before him. (Nelson's SB pg. 479)

The only likely opponent would have been King Saul since he was from his shoulders upward taller than any Israelite. (Nelson's SB pg. 479) However, he and the other Israelites were greatly afraid of their enemy. For forty days, morning and evening Goliath came with taunting jeers! Goliath not only defied the armies but more importantly their God!

Isn't that what the devil does daily in our minds? He tries to inject his poisonous darts of fear that try to steal our peace.

One day as I was praying and on the floor crying out to God I was saying, "I can't and I don't have it." I was in a situation that fear was maintaining a hold on my emotions. I heard the Lord in my spirit say, "Stand up! I have given you everything that you need. My power is within you to conquer the lies of the enemy. Look to me, my daughter, with your head held high. You are a child of the King. Do you know what that means? You are royalty! Nothing that you desire is hidden from you. I have given you my favor, anointing and blessing. See yourself strong, bold, and courageous for that is how I see you. See yourself with love pouring out of you for others for that love is in you. I am inside of you. I am love. Draw from my well of love."

He said, "Fear is blocking the love. You have been afraid of being hurt!"

One morning during my time with the Lord I saw myself in a vision. A building was on fire and I was at the top floor beginning to panic about not being able to get out. Suddenly, I heard Jesus calling my name. I looked out the window and saw Jesus with his arms stretched out to catch me. I looked around the room. The smoke was beginning to rise up to the top floor; however, when I looked outside it was quite a jump. Fear was gripping me in both situations! I wanted to jump into Jesus' arms for I knew that he was my only hope of escape! However, my fear of height was taking over and I knew that if I stayed in a burning building I would be consumed in the fire.

Suddenly, the Lord said, "I am taking you into a deeper place within your heart. You will feel my presence where you least expect me to be. My desire is to show you more of me. As I show you more of me, you will see less of you. My daughter, I am here for you. My arms are opened wide to catch you. I will not let you fall! You are safe in my arms!"

"His heart is secure, he will have no fear. In the end he will look in triumph on his foes." (Psalm 112:8 NIV)

No matter what God calls you to do there are challenges. However, when you see yourself in His arms and no longer trapped in a burning building of fear you will be able to see the confidence that God has placed within you.

It looked like no one would step up to the plate and take Goliath's challenge.

"And all the men in Israel, when they saw the man, fled from him and were dreadfully afraid." (I Samuel 17:24 NKJ)

Why were the Israelites full of fear? The Philistines stood on a mountain on one side, and Israel stood on a mountain on the other side, with a valley between them. There was a steep ravine that extended up the middle of the valley that probably prevented the Philistines from a full quick attack.

Have you ever been paralyzed with fear? Where was your focus? The Israelites focus was on the giant Goliath and not on their **undefeated Champion**! Had they forgotten what God had done for them in the past? Didn't they remember the deliverance from Egypt and the Red Sea miracle?

One day as I was talking with the Lord, I heard Him ask me this question. "Who was the Israelite's greatest enemy, the Red Sea or the Egyptians?" I said, "I don't know, Lord." He said, "Fear was their greatest enemy!"

For forty days and nights they listened to Goliath's taunts and became more terrified. Didn't they realize that God was ahead of them and would work all this out for His glory? Did anyone look at the ravine and see this as the hand of God to delay the Philistines while He worked behind the scenes?

When God began to root fear out of me, He spoke into my heart that fear is listening to satan's word and faith is listening to God's word! Those words gripped my heart! I certainly didn't want to be listening to satan's plot over God's plan!

The Lord gave me a vision of a couple in a boxing ring. Satan would speak words of fear, rejection, jealousy, anger, selfishness, pride, etc. that spurred them to put their boxing gloves on. On the other side of the ring Jesus was praying for them. In the midst of the fighting Jesus spoke words of faith, acceptance, love, peace, humility, etc. When they listened to His word, they would stop fighting. When they listened to the enemy's words they would resume the battle.

In one of our renewals in a church service, we had a drama that portrayed this as satan's plot and God's plan. At the end of the service, the Pastor said, "Today we have all seen God's word proven!"

Now, let's look at what God has been doing in this delay. God was getting ready to show Himself strong through a shepherd boy.

"So David rose early in the morning, left the sheep with a keeper, and took the things and went as Jesse had commanded him. And he came to the camp as the army was going out to fight and shouting for the battle. For Israel and the Philistines had drawn up in battle array, army against army." (I Samuel 17:20 NKJ)

First of all, David rose up early in the morning.

Rose is taken from a Hebrew word that means to incline. (Strongs)

Joshua 24:23 says, "Then put away, said He, the foreign gods that are among you and incline your hearts to the Lord, the God of Israel." (AMP)

I believe that David inclined his heart to hear from the Lord daily. When David greeted his brothers at the battle lines, he heard Goliath's defiance not only against the Israelites but against His God! Seeing his terror stricken brothers and Israelites, David's spirit rose up against this bold opposition!

One day the Lord gave me a vision of how strong our spirits are to be in the Lord. I'm sure many of you will remember the television program called "The Hulk!" Anybody who came against him was in terror! God revealed to me that the enemy was getting out all kinds of weapons to annihilate my mind, will and emotions. However, as he gave it his best shot........my spirit rose to the occasion and the artillery bounced off my spirit!

Let's take a look at what David says. "What shall be done for the man who kills this Philistine and takes away the reproach from Israel?" (I Samuel 17:14 NIV) He knew that the army was hiding like cowards and allowing the enemy to keep them in bondage. He didn't say, "If he kills him." He made a declaration of faith that it would happen. Then he said, "For who is this uncircumcised Philistine that he should defy the armies of the Living God?" (I Samuel 17:14NIV) In other words, how dare he come up against our God? Who does he think he is? David was aware of the attack and knew the nature of his enemy and exercised his authority over him. He knew and served a living God not a pagan god. He didn't see Goliath as the undefeated champion Hulk. On the contrary, David's spirit was rising like the **Hulk** and saw God as the **undefeated Champion**!

Israel is faced with a giant and they cower in fear. However, David sees it as a done deal. God is greater than this giant. He sees this as an opportunity for God to show Himself strong to His children. He has faith in His God that He will be with him to overcome the enemy.

But then another opposition comes in that's much more subtle than the Philistine Goliath............a family member. Isn't that how the enemy works in our lives? If he can't stop us one way..............he'll try those that are closest to us.

"Now Eliab his eldest brother heard what he said to the men; and Eliab's anger was kindled against David and he said, "Why did you come here? With whom have you left those few sheep in the wilderness? I know your presumption and evilness of heart; for you came down that you might see the battle." (I Samuel 17:28 AMP)

David had asked the men what would be done for the man who kills this Philistine and his brother got very angry at him.

Why was Eliab spewing those angry hurtful words to his baby brother? Perhaps David's brother was jealous. After all, he was the oldest............how would it look for his baby brother to step up to the plate?

David says.............What have I done now? Was it not a harmless question?

Whenever someone is upset with us..............don't we say, "What did I do?" David did nothing to deserve this kind of treatment. However, satan was using the weaknesses of his brother to attack the weaknesses of David!

Satan uses the weaknesses of others to combat the weaknesses in us. However, God allows this to bring His strength in the midst of our weaknesses! David knew that life is full of problem solving opportunities for God to show Himself strong to His children. David had a positive outlook and was not entrenched in a negative mindset to keep him from believing what God would accomplish through him.

What are you telling yourself and others in the midst of your problems?

God is not calling us to fight each other but to fight our enemy whose goal is to annihilate our minds.

"And David turned away from Eliab to another and he asked the same question, and again the men gave him the same answer!" (I Samuel 17:30 AMP)

Notice David turned away from his brother and focused on what God was calling him to do. David didn't listen to his brother's negative words. He didn't allow the spirit of intimidation or his brother's jealousy to crush his spirit. He turned what could have been a major disappointment into God's appointment. God was sending him on a mission. God had given him a statement of faith. How dare the Philistines defy the armies of God! He knew who he was and........ He believed his God!

Do you believe what God or others say about you?

Isaiah 52:12 says, " For you will not go out with haste, nor will you go in flight(as was necessary when Israel left Egypt); for the Lord will go before you, and the God of Israel will be your rear guard!"(AMP)

Think of that! I saw Jesus in a vision walking ahead of me..........however His foot prints were behind Him.......... He turned around to me and told me to step in and follow Him! You see, He already has walked ahead of everything that we will experience in this journey!

Jeremiah 23:23 says, "Am I a God near at hand, says the Lord, and Not a God afar off?"(NIV)

Can you imagine the buzz around the city? "Have you heard the latest....there is a little shepherd boy boasting that he will slay the Philistine giant. You've got to be kidding............the whole army is living in fear. C'mon you are telling us that Eliab's baby brother is volunteering for this mission? Who does he think he is? Well, this I've got to see. I can't wait to see the expression on Saul's face when he hears this. He probably needs a good belly laugh!"

Finally the news reached Saul and he summoned David to speak to him.

David said to Saul, "Let no man's heart fail because of this Philistine; your servant will go out and fight with him." (I Samuel 17: 32 AMP)

Can you imagine the thoughts running through Saul's mind while looking at this little shepherd boy's stature? What is this a joke that is being played on me? Saul could not see that this little shepherd boy with no training in the army could fight such a powerful enemy. After all he is only a youth and the Philistine giant has been a warrior from his youth. However, he was looking at the outward appearance and not seeing the spirit that was in David.

David recalled the story of the lion and the bear he killed while protecting his sheep knowing that God delivered him out of their paws and knew that he would deliver him out of the hand of the enemy. What were Saul's thoughts now? Perhaps, "I'm the King and I can't get rid of this nagging fear yet............ I hear no fear in David. How can he be so bold?"

"And Saul said to David, Go and the Lord be with you." (I Samuel 17:37 AMP)

What changed Saul's mind? I believe that he heard the spirit of God and the authority that God had given to David to speak His words. He no longer focused on what David couldn't do but what God could do through David.

Maybe you are in a situation that looks overwhelming! Begin to recall how God has delivered you out of situations in the past. You serve a living God! He isn't dead. Begin to declare His word over your life as David did.

David not only had his focus on God, he believed that God would deliver him from the hand of the enemy. He placed his confidence in God and spoke with authority over the circumstance.

On the day of the battle David knew the battle was not his but the Lord's!

I Samuel 17:45 says, "You come against me with sword and spear and javelin, but I come against you in the name of the Lord Almighty, the God of the armies of Israel, whom you have defied. This day the Lord will hand you over to me and I'll strike you down and cut off your head. Today I will give the carcasses of the Philistine army to the birds of the air and the beasts of the earth and the whole world will know that there is a great God in Israel. All those gathered here will know that it is not by sword or spear that the Lord saves; for the battle is the Lord's and He will give all of you into our hands." (NIV)

Wow! Can you comprehend what David was saying! David was bragging on His God. Can you hear God bragging on David? "That's my boy! Hey, Angels, come listen to what my son says! He believes me when I speak. Way to go, David! This is what I've been waiting for! Now I can show myself strong to my children!"

David wasn't boasting of himself but had humbled himself and boasted about His God, knowing that the battle was in the Lord's hands.

"Therefore, as it is written, let him who boasts and proudly rejoices and glories, boast and proudly rejoice and glory in the Lord." (I Corinthians 1:31AMP)

David didn't see himself as a victim but saw his God as the Victor!

Psalm 119:114 says, "You are my hiding place and my shield. I hope in your word." (AMP)

David carried the shield of God and knew that He was his hiding place. It was just the opposite for the Israelite army who carried physical weapons but did not see God as their shield which caused them to hide within their fears!

Have you ever had a day that you wanted to crawl back into bed and hide under the covers and never come out? Well, I've had some of those days.

On one of those days, the Lord told me that I was hiding within myself instead of making Him my hiding place!

We all have a choice. Are we going to take God at His word or allow the enemy to place fear, doubt and unbelief in our minds?

When I stopped hiding my weaknesses and became real with God, He became my safe **Hiding Place** and I received my daddy's open arms of love! I felt His peace in the midst of the trials in my life and He became my shield and protector.

We all have hidden secrets in the closets of our hearts but we need to stop using our past as an excuse to remain a victim of satan and allow God to make our past His opportunity to propel us to Victory and the plan that He has for our life! How long has it been since you have bragged on your **undefeated Champion**?

New

As this beautiful woman looks into the mirror, she can only see herself as not pretty enough, smart enough or good enough. She notices every flaw an imperfection. She cannot see what God sees because her focus is on herself.

Because of the weaknesses within herself, the enemy bombards her mind with discouragement and she doesn't realize that if she gives those weaknesses to God, He will perfect them.

She sees herself as a reject and projects that expectation on to others that they will reject her too.

The makeup conceals the wrinkles and blemishes on her face but doesn't touch the wrinkles and blemishes of her past. She has pain hidden in the depths of her heart and needs her Savior to pull her up out of the garbage that has been accumulated over many years. Because she is focused on herself and what's wrong with her, she doesn't see that she is in right standing with God because of the price Jesus paid in shedding His blood to free her from the shackles of sin. Jesus gave His life for her so that she might live an abundant life with Him!

She has unforgiveness in her heart but feels that she is right in staying angry. After all, it wasn't her fault!

She lives day by day existing with anxiousness and fear of her future. She doesn't realize that perfect love casts out fear and that she is to cast all of her cares on Jesus because He loves her so much. She continues to carry the burdens of life not laying them at Jesus feet.

Oh, by the way..........did I mention that she goes to church every Sunday and Wednesday evening. She also teaches and is very active. She worships the Lord with her lips but not with her heart. She really hopes that it will be a good message today since she really needs it. Yet, it's never enough so she goes home and lives her mundane life. She doesn't realize that she needs a personal relationship with God and that He is waiting with open arms for her to sit in His presence daily! She doesn't realize that God has fresh manna for her............in other words, His divine words of guidance, direction and encouragement for her day ahead.

She has been told that God has a plan and purpose for her life but she feels that God has forgotten her.

She looks around at gifts in others from God but doesn't realize the gifts within herself since they are covered up by all the pain in the closet of her heart.

Does she sound familiar? Do you know anyone like her? Perhaps she sounds like you. This woman was me!

Remember the nursery rhyme "Humpty Dumpty" that says "Humpty Dumpty sat on a wall. Humpty Dumpty had a great fall. All of the King's horses and all of the King's men could not put Humpty Dumpty back together again."

God spoke in my heart that He was the only one who could put me back together again. Many of you have had your hearts broken into pieces and you can hardly function because of so much pain! Your daddy is here to help you pick up the pieces and put you back together!

I am reminded of a program on television where they attempt to make women look at least ten years younger in a matter of weeks.

I've watched how they are given a complete transformation that includes a new hairdo, makeup, teeth repair and whitening, and new outfits that are stylish. They even send a trainer along to work an extensive exercise program. If the weight is down far enough, they qualify for surgery to perfect certain areas of their bodies.

The day finally comes when they are paraded in front of everyone to see their amazing transformation. Their friends and family barely know them and they are so excited to see their new look!

However, I've always wondered how long they keep that new look!

Okay, they look beautiful on the outside but what about the inside?

What baggage are they carrying that caused them to get like this in the first place? Are they carrying anger, fear, unforgiveness, worry, doubt, jealousy, etc.? What void in their hearts are they trying to fill?

If these women could be turned inside out and we could see the real woman, what would we see?

If I ask you the question "Do you like yourself?" how many of you would say "yes" without any hesitation? In 1998 I started a women's weight loss group in our home. As we met together we realized that none of us liked ourselves and that we had very low self esteem. We carried emotional weight that brought us to not only gain the weight but fail in losing it.

One day as we were praying, the Lord gave me a vision of a heart with many pieces in it like a puzzle. Beside the heart was a bag of presents. The Lord said, "As you give me the pieces of your hearts such as.......... anger, unforgiveness, pride, jealousy, etc.........the blessings will come such as............. love, peace, joy, etc."

"Galatians 5:22 says, "but the fruit of the spirit is love, joy, peace, longsuffering, gentleness, goodness, faith, meekness, temperance: against such there is no law." (NIV) The Amplified Bible says, "But the fruit of the Holy Spirit (The work which His presence within accomplishes)!"

Did you catch that? The Holy Spirit's presence within you does the work in your heart.............not you trying to change yourself.

One night I had a dream of many women that were trying to change themselves. They were so frustrated and stressed out because they couldn't get the results that they so desired. I told them you can't change yourself but when you begin to have a relationship with our Lord...........He will begin to change what you cannot change.

One day I drove up to the top of one of our mountains and screamed and wept before the Lord and asked Him what was wrong with me. I said, "I can't do this anymore. I've tried to change myself but I can't." I heard the Lord say, "That's right you can't..... But I can. This is what I have been waiting for, now I can work!"

God was waiting for me to give all my heart and mind to Him. When we stay in that mentality we continue to hold on to the darkness in our hearts and never experience the joy that God has for us.

"Psalm 139:23 says, "Search me O God and know my heart, test me and know my anxious thoughts. See if there is any offensive way in me and lead me in the way everlasting." (NIV)

As I began to pray this scripture daily, God began to reveal areas in my heart that needed to be healed. I learned to lay them at Jesus feet and ask Him to change me. As I opened the door of the closet of my heart that contained fear, unforgiveness, selfishness and pride, God began a new work in me.

When we have an appointment with a physician we inform him of our symptoms. Sometimes he sends us to a hospital for x-rays to see if anything is broken, any diseased areas such as cardio vascular or infections in the body. After the x-rays are taken, the doctor places them on a screen that has a light and begins to review the areas that might need some surgery or some other treatment. Some areas may require extensive surgery or out patient surgery while others may only require medication! When you tell the doctor your symptoms, he looks for the root cause and moves you towards a cure. You wouldn't walk into the doctor's office and give him the cure because you only know the symptoms, right?

Well, you have Dr. Jesus at any time to talk with about your symptoms. As you make an appointment with the doctor, God waits for you to take time with Him. God knows what areas are deep rooted and need His surgery and other areas that need His medication.

Think of the latest exercise equipment. Many people buy them and have good intentions of keeping up the exercises, however; pain begins to show up in muscles that aren't used to the work and eventually the newness wears off and the excuses take over. When we ask the Lord to change our hearts, He begins a process that leads to pulling out the root cause and bringing the hidden pain to the surface. We have a choice! Will we allow God to do the surgery that is needed or run from the pain and continue stuffing our emotions? We can choose to exercise our faith muscle and see the newness of God daily or we can choose to let the newness of God wear off and allow the excuses to take over!

We can't change ourselves, but we can give ourselves completely to Him and watch the potter at work as He masters over the clay.

One day I was praying for someone and saw Jesus hands kneading dough. As He was working on the dough, there was a pie plate beside it. The dough was being prepared to fit in the pie plate just right.

The definition of kneading is to mix and work dough or clay into a uniform mass usually by pressing and pulling with the hands. To work upon by squeezes of the hands, massage. (Funk and Wagnall)

When we allow God to examine our hearts, He pulls, presses, squeezes and pats us, making us fit for the Master's plan! We become His hand crafted work of art created by the Master Craftsman!

As God began this process in me, He told me to face the pain. I saw Him in a vision holding a key to unlock a door of fear inside my heart. He spoke these words, "Quiet your heart and mind before me. I give you my heart and my eyes to see what only I can see. When you look to me you will see yourself and others through my eyes. My eyes are not dim like your natural eyes. I see your heart. I know what your deep cries are. When you look and rely on me then you will see deep inside your heart what you do not know. I love you with an everlasting love. My love is greater than you could ever imagine. You are my little girl. Come and sit on my lap. Lay your head on my shoulder and cry those tears that you have held back for so long. Let me cleanse you and free you from this deep deep deep pain!"

Perhaps, as you are reading this, you can feel God touching you. Stop and review this word from the Lord. He wants to unlock the door of your heart and He is the only one who holds the key! You are His little child and He wants to free you from this deep pain that you have carried for many years.

Open up your heart and allow your Father to shine His light on those areas of your heart that have been wounded.

"This is the message that we have heard from Him and declare to you. God is light; in Him there is no darkness at all. If we claim to have fellowship with Him yet walk in darkness, we lie and do not live by the truth. But if we walk in the light, as He is in the light, we have fellowship with one another and the blood of Jesus, His son, purifies us from all sin. If we claim to be without sin, we deceive ourselves and the truth is not in us. If we confess our sins, He is faithful and just to forgive us our sins and purify us from all unrighteousness. If we claim we have not sinned, we make Him out to be a liar and His word has no place in our lives." (I John 1:5-10 NIV)

In 2001 I asked the Lord to shine His light on the dark areas in my life. He showed me unforgiveness in my heart towards my dad. My dad was strict and was a very serious man. He wasn't one to express his emotions and never told me that he loved me. I called him the warden and really felt that he was. Because my focus was on my dad meeting **my** emotional needs, I failed to look at all **his** attributes. I was a prisoner of the fear of him. I had certain expectations of how my dad should love me. Because he wasn't able emotionally to show that love I had judged his love for me. The day the Lord showed me the unforgiveness in my heart; I took a pen and paper and prayed for all the situations in which I had unforgiveness. I wrote each one of them and then lifted them up to the Lord and said the words, "I forgive." I didn't forgive him because I felt like it; I forgave him because I chose to obey God.

April 1, 2003 my mother called to let me know that the doctor found a mass on my dad's esophagus and she would call me later with the results. Later my brother told me they found a mass on my dad's esophagus about the size of a dime. That evening during the service at our church, the Holy Spirit moved on my heart. I went up to the altar and wept and wept. God began a work on rooting out the pain of so many years. My pastor prayed that every hurtful word that was said over me would be healed. I could feel God softening my heart.

He gave me a vision of myself coming out of a sewer. He showed me that all this garbage was buried inside of me. I had crawled underground in my emotions and had put the lid on. Now I was coming up quickly from being buried under all this excretion of pain and suffering and was taking the lid off! It was no longer buried because I was allowing God to take control of this dark area in my heart.

"They have greatly oppressed me from my youth. Let Israel say they have greatly oppressed me from my youth but they have not gained victory over me. Plowmen have plowed my back and made their furrows long. But the Lord is righteous. He has cut me free from the cords of the wicked." (Psalm 129:1-4 NIV)

Furrow is a narrow channel made in the ground by or as if by a plow; any long, narrow, deep depression as a groove, rut or deep wrinkle. (Funk and Wagnall)

God was beginning to remove those wrinkles!

Two weeks later I was taking my mother out to lunch and felt God was saying to pray with my dad. I had prayed for my dad but never with my dad. My first thought was I didn't hear that right! Isn't that what we do when we don't want to do what God says? Come on now, be honest! However, God was way ahead of me. As I was trying to shrug it off, my mother said, "There is something that I would like you to do. I'd like you to pray with Dad and me." When we got back to the house, Dad was watching television. I told him that I would like to pray with them if he wanted me too. He immediately turned the television off. I took my mother and dad's hand and lifted them up to the Lord. As I was praying for them, the power of God came on us that caused our hands to shake. When the prayer ended, for the first time in my life, I had no fear. I looked at my dad and had an overwhelming love for him.

In those next weeks I had the privilege of being with my dad. My dad had accepted Jesus into his heart years ago. I was able to tell my dad that I loved him and feel it. I am so thankful that God gave me those precious weeks without fear that was covering up the love in my heart.

"There is no fear in love (dread does not exist), but full-grown (complete, perfect) love turns fear out of doors and expels every trace of terror! For fear brings with it the thought of punishment and (so) he who is afraid has not reached the full maturity of love (is not yet grown into love's complete perfection)." (I John 4:18 AMP)

Remember the vision that I had of Jesus with a key to open the door of fear? He took that key and unlocked the door and expelled every trace of terror in me. I believe that God started this process when I made the choice to forgive my dad two years before his illness.

Sometimes our loved ones die suddenly and we don't get a second chance. God gave me that second chance and I am so grateful!

When my dad was moved to the nursing home because the pain was too great, he told me that he was scared. I read from Isaiah 44 that says, "He, who made you, who formed you in the womb and will help you. Do not be afraid." (NIV) During those last weeks, I was able to pray with Mom and Dad, prop his pillow, read to him and tell him how important he was to me and that I loved him. One day when Dad could barely talk, he said, "Pray for me." I said, "I am." He said, "Now! I want to go home!" I took my mom and dad's hand and lifted him up to Jesus. I asked the Lord to take my dad home quickly and help us let go of him.

Four days before my dad went home, I had a dream. I saw my dad in the hospice room getting quickly out of his bed. I saw that he no longer had rheumatoid arthritis, leukemia or cancer. He walked to the edge of the room and then disappeared. I felt such a peace in that dream and I knew God was coming to take my dad home soon.

June 28, 2003, my husband, Mom and I were with Dad. He no longer was eating or drinking and couldn't respond. A hospice nurse came into the room and told us that she wanted to help make this a beautiful experience. We were looking at my dad and each other not knowing what to do. She said he can't respond but he hears everything you are saying. I sat on the bed and talked to him about heaven. I told him about the dream that God had given me. I told him that he was totally healed and would never have these illnesses again. We are so grateful to his nurse that encouraged us to make this a beautiful experience on his last day on earth. Later that evening I played a CD that was on the table in his room. It was called, "New World in the Morning!" Before I left the room, I took my mom and dad's hand and thanked God for taking my dad quickly. For the first time that day, my dad looked me in the eyes as I said, "Jesus is coming for you and you're going to have joy in the morning!" I had not known that Jesus was coming for him in two hours!

The next morning I was getting ready to meet with our family and Dad's pastor. The Lord said, "I've got your daddy. He is in my arms!" He truly is a Sovereign God! I had the privilege to speak and sing at my dad's service. The song I sang was called, "NO MORE PAIN!"
(Lyrics by Geoff Thurman, Becky Thurman and Michael English)

Are you holding any unforgiveness in your heart? Open up your heart and allow God to reveal any areas that have been wounded.

Forgiveness is granting pardon for or remission of something; to cease to blame or feel resentment against. (Funk and Wagnall)

We can choose to forgive or hold unforgiveness in our heart that cause a root of bitterness. It's our choice of being bitter or better!

My husband had been remodeling our family room. He removed all the old carpet from our steps and my job was to scrub them. As I was scrubbing, I felt something jab my finger. Sure enough there was a splinter. I was in such a hurry to finish up that I didn't take the time to remove it. Since I didn't feel anymore pain I ignored it. The next day I noticed redness all around the area of the splinter. When I touched my finger I could feel some pain. By the next day I noticed that it was beginning to get infected. Now it was going to be even more painful to remove since the splinter had lodged in my skin. The Lord spoke into my heart that this is what happens when we don't forgive immediately! In the beginning the offense hurts but we allow it to move into our hearts and fester. When we continue to internalize the unforgiveness it becomes a root of bitterness and the pain is hidden. When we allow the Holy Spirit to begin His work on the darkness of unforgiveness the pain is revealed and no longer remains. The power of God heals those wounds of the past.

"Let all bitterness and indignation and wrath (passion, rage, bad temper) and resentment (anger, animosity) and quarreling (brawling, clamor, contention) and slander (evil speaking, abusive or blasphemous language) be banished (from you, with all malice (spite, ill will, or baseness of any kind). And become useful and helpful and kind to one another, tender hearted (compassionate, understanding, loving-hearted), forgiving one another (readily and freely), as God in Christ forgave you." (Ephesians 4:31-32 AMP)

Notice the end of that verse says forgiving one another **readily** and **freely**! I can hear some of you saying. "Jenny, you don't know how much I've been hurt when I didn't deserve it!"

Forgiveness doesn't mean what the person said or did is ok! It's making a choice to obey God. It allows Him to break satan's destructive hold and frees God to restore you emotionally and spiritually. Forgiveness also allows God's hand to work in your life. It removes dead weight and gives you back your life. Forgiveness is letting go of the offense and no longer being justified in your anger.

It's giving up the right to hurt the other person back. It's not waiting for the other person to say they are sorry and then you forgive.

I was watching a program on television. The main character's husband had left her for another woman and she said, "I can only forgive you if you say you are sorry." He said, "I'm not, I'm happy. You'll just have to deal with it." Many times we will not get a sorry from the other person.

In one of our renewals, I had shared these words and a lady spoke up and told me that she had been told to deal with it. That day she forgave that person after many years of holding those painful words in her heart and rededicated her life to the Lord! Praise God! He is faithful!

In another of our renewals I had been teaching on forgiveness. Afterwards, we prayed that God would reveal any unforgiveness in our hearts. As we asked the Holy Spirit to shine His light on that dark area, we made a list of people that He revealed that had hurt us and the offense. We made the choice to forgive. One of the ladies brought her list up front of the past wounds by her father. She chose to forgive each offense and then ripped it up! I watched as her countenance changed from when she first entered the room. I saw a joyful expression on her face and her eyes sparkled. Praise God! He broke that bondage of so many years!

Forgiveness is not three strikes and you are out!

"Then Peter came to Jesus and asked, Lord, how many times shall I forgive my brother when he sins against me? Up to seventy times? Jesus answered I tell you, not seven times but seventy times seven." (Matthew 18:21-22 NIV)

In other words, we are to forgive all the time!

"But if you do not forgive men their sins, your Father will not forgive your sins." (Matthew 6:15 NIV)

Matthew 5:23-24 says, "Therefore, if you are offering your gift at the altar and there remember that your brother has something against you, leave your gift at the front of the altar. First go and be reconciled with your brother, then come and offer your gift." (NIV)

I believe God is more interested in the reconciliation with people than He is in sacrifices or good works such as teaching Sunday school or Bible studies, being on the worship team, being a board member, or even being a minister. God is in the ministry of reconciliation!

When God tells you to reconcile with that person you are not responsible for their reaction. You are responsible to obey God and the rest is up to Him!

"The heart is deceitful above all things and desperately wicked; who can know it?" (Jeremiah 17:9 NKJ)

Until we allow God to examine our hearts we are not fully aware of the areas of unforgiveness. One morning I was asking the Lord to search my heart for any unforgiveness in me. Later that day my mother, son and I had been in another county shopping mall. My son noticed a woman that I had not seen for many years. My immediate response was, "Oh great!" Immediately, the Holy Spirit pricked my heart and revealed unforgiveness towards her for a situation that I had gone through in the past. I hadn't thought of her in years, yet the wound was still in my heart! As soon as this was revealed to me, I immediately chose to forgive her. Months later I saw her again in another shopping mall. I felt like the situation had never taken place. Praise God! When I made the choice to forgive, God healed my pain and changed my heart.

In my first marriage I experienced intense jealousy and cried out for God's help!

He spoke these words into my spirit. "I want you to separate the sin from the person! Look at her with my eyes! I love her as much as I love you." I felt His presence of love wrapped around me like a cloak. Immediately, I chose to forgive her and asked the Lord to forgive me. After all, if God separated her sin and loved her as much as me.................who am I to look at her sin? I no longer was focused on her and my problems but felt renewed, restored and rejuvenated in my mind and my heart.

Maybe you have done something in your life that has caused you to live under shame and guilt.

Gen 45:5 says, "And now do not be distressed and do not be angry with yourselves for sending me here because it was to save lives that God sent me ahead of you." (NIV)

Joseph was telling his brothers that they needed to forgive themselves for selling him out. What satan meant for evil, God turned for Joseph's good and God's glory!

One of my favorite television programs has been "Little House on the Prairie" for many years. One day as I was watching the program, a Jewish man was being mocked and ridiculed for his faith. Charles Ingles stood up and befriended this man against the whole town. Suddenly the Holy Spirit moved on my heart and I began to weep and weep. A scene flashed before me of when I was in High School. We had a Jewish girl in our class that most everyone rejected and ridiculed because of her faith. I never treated her badly or even talked about her, however; I never stood up against the other classmates. The Holy Spirit brought conviction upon me and I repented of the fear that kept me silent. I told the Lord if He would bring her into my path I would tell her that I was sorry. God took my vow seriously! A couple of days later my mother and I were in a shopping mall in Lancaster. I had a part that needed replaced on one of our appliances. I couldn't believe my eyes! God had led me straight to her. She was busy with other customers and more were waiting in line. I could have looked at this scenario and decided that she was too busy............instead I asked the Holy Spirit what to do. He told me to wait until everyone was waited on. My mother and I walked around for awhile and waited. Finally I was the last in line. As we talked she thought I looked familiar! Now you need to understand that I had not seen her for about forty years. I told her how the Holy Spirit moved on my heart while watching the television program and convicted me for not standing up for her. I felt the pain in her as we hugged and cried together! Praise God! He showed Himself strong to both of us. God saw the pain that this lady has suffered for many years and convicted my heart to repent and brought forgiveness and healing to both of us.

"There is therefore now no condemnation to those who are in Jesus Christ." (Romans 8:1 NKJ)

One day I was outside under our tree having my time with the Lord. All of a sudden I heard a woodpecker. It was beginning to annoy me since I wanted to sit in silence and hear God's voice. The Lord said, "This is what the enemy does to my children. He pecks at their minds continually with thoughts of what they did wrong. I have called my children to not look at what they have done but what I have already accomplished and can do through them when they give their hearts fully to me."

I beat myself up in my thoughts for many months during the separation until God began to cleanse my mind as I sat in His presence!

Imagine a tank full of dirt that piles up over the years if not cleaned out. If the heart is not cleansed, the dirt continues to pile up and becomes like grit.

The Lord gave me a vision of a clogged pipe. He showed me that the pipe was so clogged that even Drano couldn't penetrate it. When we give God the unforgiveness of ourselves and others, God's Drano of love penetrates that hardness and we begin to feel His love surrounding us for ourselves and others!

As I pray with many women, I have noticed a lot of dirty laundry piling upon God's children. Many times we take the responsibility for someone else's actions. As long as we allow the enemy to pile others' dirty laundry on us...........that person doesn't get set free! In other words, we become enablers! They need to come into accountability for their actions and words! If you keep trying to hold them together, you will fall apart! You are created by God and so are they. It is His responsibility to change them and their responsibility to allow that change!

One day I was telling God that I felt that I messed up in allowing thoughts into my mind that I shouldn't have. I heard Him say ever so gently to me, "But you have a heart for me." I could actually see Him smiling at me! You see, even when we mess up, God knows that we are trying and our daddy sees our heart!

"For if our heart condemns us God is greater than our heart and knows all things. We recognize that we do not measure up to the standard of love and feel insecure in approaching God. God takes everything into account, including Jesus atonement." (I John 3:20 NKJ)

"Blessed is he whose transgression is forgiven, whose sin is covered. Blessed is the man to whom the Lord does not impute iniquity and in whose spirit there is no deceit." (Psalm 32:1-2 NKJ)

King David had resisted his admission of guilt in his affair with Bathsheba, hoping that in time the sin and its consequence would go away. God kept a heavy hand upon David to bring him into repentance which caused great agony emotionally, physically and spiritually!

"When I kept silent (before I confessed), my bones wasted away through my groaning all the day long. For day and night your hand (of displeasure) was heavy upon me; my moisture was turned into the drought of summer." (Psalm 32:3-4 AMP)

When God sent Nathan the prophet to reveal David's sin, He brought David to confess and repent of his sins.

Have you given up trying to follow God? Do you believe that God will never forgive you? Do you believe that God wants to give you an abundant life? Is the guilt self inflicted or are you carrying other people's judgment or criticism? Are you tired of carrying this shame? Are you ready to lay your burdens down and begin a fresh start?

No matter what you've done, it's not hopeless. Jesus is here today with His arms stretched out to you to offer His forgiveness to you. As long as the unforgiveness remains the enemy has a weapon formed against you.

"But no weapon that is formed against you shall prosper, and every tongue that shall rise against you in judgment, you shall show to be in the wrong. This (peace, righteousness, security, triumph over opposition) is the heritage of the servants of the Lord (those in whom the ideal Servant of the Lord is produced) this is the righteousness or the vindication which they obtain from me (this is that which I impart to them as justification), says the Lord." (Isaiah 54:17 AMP)

Okay, now that you have allowed God to root out unforgiveness towards yourself and others, how do you stay free?

"Psalm 26:2 says, "Test me, O Lord and try me, examine my heart and my mind for your love is ever before me and I walk continually in your truth." (NIV)

Immediately, when someone does or says something to you or about you........choose to forgive them and thank God that He has created a clean heart in both of you. By doing this and asking God daily to examine your heart, you won't develop that root.

When Jesus was on the cross He said, "Father forgive them for they know not what they do."

Sometimes people are just very insensitive and you need to forgive them for their insensitivity. Not all people are down right malicious. They are blinded by the darkness of satan and the sins that are in their heart.

"Therefore, if any person is (in grafted) in Christ (the Messiah) he is a **new** creation (a new creature altogether); the old (previous moral and spiritual condition) has passed away. Behold! The fresh and **new** have come." (II Corinthians 5:17 AMP)

The definition of **new** is...... different from that which is older or previous, fresh, unspoiled, renewed, rejuvenated and refreshed. (Funk and Wagnall)

C'mon let's get excited over God's word!

One morning during worship in our church, the Lord gave me a vision. I saw myself under a shower with my head back so as not to get my hair wet. God spoke in my heart that He wanted to cleanse all of me..........not just certain areas. He encouraged me to step under His shower!

"As far as the east is from the west, so far has He removed our transgressions from us." (Psalm 103:12 AMP)

Are you going through the motions of living day by day? When disappointments come into your life, how do you react?

The Lord spoke this in my heart. "Whatever I have appointed you to do.........do not look at the disappointments along the way. Look only at my appointments. I will clear the path as long as you stay humble before me with a willing heart to serve me no matter what. Know that I am your Master, Guide and Director."

At this point He gave me this vision. I saw a choir with a Director leading them. Each person knew when to sing louder or softer. They knew when to take a break or stop. They also knew when it was time for the next song. The Lord said, "My children need to see me as the director of their lives. I give the cue when to slow down, keep going, take a break or stop so I can take them another direction."

When you look into a mirror do you see anger, fear, unforgiveness, selfishness, rejection or pride?

When Jesus came into your life, His plan was to release you from confinements or restrictions of the past, negative mind sets and liberated from jealousies, unforgiveness, selfishness, pride, anger, fear, and rejection.

Liberated is defined as to set free as from bondage or confinement; to extricate as entanglement. (Funk and Wagnall)

One day as I was praying, the Lord gave me this vision. I saw a large ball of yarn. Suddenly a cat had the ball of yarn in between his paws. As the cat played with the yarn, it became more tangled. The Lord spoke this in my heart. "Oh, what a tangled web we weave!"

Tangled means to twist or involve in a confused and not readily separable mass; a state of perplexity or bewilderment.(Funk and Wagnall)

When we try to unravel things we weave a tangled mess. When we give the tangled mess to God..................He unravels the mess and it is finished!

Perhaps you have a tangled mess of many years and have tried to unravel all the confused mass of pain and suffering in you and......... or your family.

One day as I was seeking the Lord for a difficult situation in my life, the Lord spoke this in my heart.

"Lay hold of the siege." One of the definitions of lay is to render ineffective; quell. Quell is to extinguish or suppress by force. Hold is to take and keep, clasp, to keep under control. (Funk and Wagnall) As I meditated on this word from the Lord, He took me to this scripture. "Blessed be the Lord! He has shown me His marvelous loving favor when I was beset as in a besieged city." (Psalm 31:21 AMP)

The definition of beset is to attack on all sides; harass, to hem in, encircle. (Funk and Wagnall)

Siege is the act of surrounding any fortified area with the intention of capturing it.......the time during which one undergoes a protracted illness or difficulty. (Funk and Wagnall)

God began to show me that we render satan's power ineffective by locating a scene, action, thought or word that enables the enemy to set up a fortified area (stronghold) with the intention of capturing our minds, will and emotions while undergoing a difficult time or trial in our lives.

I asked the Lord how to render satan's power ineffective. He showed me to write down painful scenes pictured in my mind, hurtful words that have been spoken over me, actions of others that have grieved me, and other thoughts of the past, present and future that plague me. The camera in my mind was continually rewinding painful pictures along with voices of the past and present. I chose to forgive and to thank the Lord for His presence. I repented of my sins and pleaded the blood of Jesus over my mind, will and emotions. I conceded to God's truth, let go of the encumbrances and resisted the devil's lies. Two days later a situation came up in which I felt disrespected. I no longer felt the anger but began to feel tears welling up within me. Suddenly I wept almost uncontrollably and grabbed hold of my body filled with emotional pain. As quickly as the weeping came...........it left within seconds. Afterwards, I felt a freedom in my emotions and was extricated from the entanglement in my mind, will and emotions. God showed His marvelous loving favor in the midst of this difficulty by unveiling the emotional pain within me.

"For though we walk in the flesh we do not war after the flesh for the weapons of our warfare are not carnal but mighty through God to the pulling down of strongholds. Casting down imaginations and every high thing that exalts itself against the knowledge of God and bringing into captivity every thought to the obedience of Christ and having a readiness to revenge all disobedience when your obedience is fulfilled." (II Corinthians 10: 3-6 KJV)

God can unravel all those years of pain and torment in one minute. He wants to restore, renew and revive your hearts today! He wants to turn your problems into possibilities! Are you ready to have your wounds replaced with God's message of healing and restoration; fear replaced with love; anger turned into forgiveness and despair turned into faith and hope?

Ask God to help you separate the sin from the person, look at them through His eyes and begin to feel the love that He has for you and the other person!

Step out of the shadows of your past and allow God to part the deep waters. Step into the waters of forgiveness and receive God's flowing mercies today!

Daring

Daring means to be brave and adventurous. (Funk and Wagnall)

Are you ready to go on an adventure that will lead you places that you have never been? If so, come with me and let's dare to take God at His word!

"So shall My word be that goes forth out of My mouth; it shall not return to Me void (without producing any effect, useless), but it shall accomplish that which I please and purpose, and it shall prosper in the thing for which I sent it." (Isaiah 55:11 AMP)

We begin walking the path that Jesus calls us to with all the comforts of home. However, when trials begin to come, our foundation begins to shake. Will we choose the choice delicacies of satan that cause us to bite off more than we can chew and be enticed with his pretty packages without seeing the full content of the consequences ahead ? Are we going to stand on God's foundations of truth or are we going to believe the lies of the enemy?

One day God spoke to me about a particular situation. He said, "They are afraid what other people will think but they don't care what I think!" I could feel His heart breaking for them.

I was going through some tough situations and was finding myself tempted to sit in self pity.

I heard the Lord say to me, "Are you going to choose to feed your flesh or your spirit today? When you allow yourself to entertain these thoughts you feed your flesh with the negativity of doubt and unbelief and self pity. When you choose to praise me and speak my word over your situations you feed your spirit! Will you choose life in the spirit and death to the flesh? Or will you choose death to your spirit and life to the flesh?"

Flesh doesn't die without putting up a fight! My flesh wanted to take control over my spirit by feeling sorry for myself. It wanted to sit in a dark corner and just stare and not read or say anything! God has created man to live in the spirit. When our journey on earth has ended, the flesh will die and the spirit will live on in heaven or in hell. It's our choice!

God gives us a choice to choose His food of love, peace, joy, meekness, patience, kindness, gentleness; goodness and self control which are His fruits that He wants to serve us daily!

One day as I was praying, I had a vision of Jesus coming behind me with a large tray of food! He put the tray in front of me that wasn't enticing like satan's pretty packages yet so delicately placed before me with His skill of excellence. Now it was my choice to eat it!

"O taste and see that the Lord (our God) is good! Blessed (happy, fortunate, to be envied) is the man who trusts and takes refuge in Him." (Psalm 34:8AMP)

Just as we must choose daily to nourish our bodies, we must choose His food for our spiritual nourishment! Instead of choosing foods that make us feel sluggish and eventually cause us to be unhealthy, we must choose foods that help us to be more alert, give us energy and make our bones stronger.

We also have a choice........ feed our flesh and allow the negativity to remain which produces a depressed state in our emotions or......... feed our spirits with the word which lifts our spirits to affect His power.

When we choose to feed our spirit, it begins to soar and take residence over the flesh which begins to starve and eventually dies.

"So then those who are living the life of the flesh (catering to the appetites and impulses of their carnal nature cannot please or satisfy God or be acceptable to Him!" (Romans 8:8 AMP)

Cater means to provide for the gratification of any needs or food! (Funk and Wagnall)

I knew that God was telling me that I had a choice to stay in self pity or meditate and speak His words of truth for my situation!

I am thankful to say I chose to cater to God's truth instead of the lie of the enemy!

"He is wooing you from the jaws of distress, to a spacious place free from restriction, to the comfort of your table laden with choice food!" (Job 36:16 NIV)

Choice food is a well selected supply, excellence, chosen with care; delicacy. (Funk and Wagnall)

Choice is a right or privilege. In other words, God gives us the privilege of choosing His delicacy which is the word of God that woos us from the jaws of distress from the enemy.

Are you going through an affliction that has placed you into a restriction? Are you sitting in a dark room of negativity and catering to your flesh?

The definition of restriction is.............limited, confined, to hold or keep within limits. (Funk and Wagnall)

In other words, what ever affliction you are going through, when you spend time in His presence and read His word, He will free you from the distress of life. You will no longer be limited or confined in your mind catering to the needs of your flesh which bring doubt, worry, anxiousness, guilt or discouragement.

Through His word served daily, we are no longer under the enemy's restrictions but receive the prescription for God's truth that frees us from all bondages!

Psalm 17:8 says, "Keep me as the apple of your eye; hide me in the shadow of your wings." (NIV)

But..........you say, "How can I be the apple of God's eye? How can He love me so much when I don't deserve His love?"

One Sunday morning it had been raining all the way to church. Needless to say, our church's front porch was decked out in all colors of the rainbow of umbrellas. My husband placed mine along with the others. After the service we were the next to the last ones to leave. There was only one black umbrella left where he had placed mine. I looked all over the porch, however mine was gone.

My umbrella had a button to touch that would cause it to open automatically! I really liked its performance and when I opened her up she was smooth. She was the Cadillac of all umbrellas. She never got stuck in the wind or rain. I knew that she would never let me down and would be my covering to keep me from getting wet. She never got bent or out of shape! She was beautiful and served me well. She was a beautiful picture of perfection!

You can imagine my shock when she was gone and another one was in her place. There was no touch button on her and she looked like she had been through the mill. She wasn't smooth when I opened her up and sometimes she would get stuck. Actually, I had to be careful that she didn't pinch my fingers. When I looked inside of her she was ugly and worn. She was not the beautiful picture of perfection and she looked like she came from a Dollar store. She certainly didn't look like she would hold up in the wind and rain without getting bent or out of shape. I knew that she would fail in serving me well. Since there was no touch button she couldn't operate without me!

Then I realized this is how God sees us! He created us with weaknesses so we would learn to depend upon Him!

One day I was watching a television program called, "Touched by an Angel." Monica, one of the angels was being blasted by an angry man's hurtful words. She didn't let her emotions run away and was able to love him in the midst of the anger. I wept before the Lord and told Him that I didn't want any other emotion… ……..I just wanted to love everybody.

Later, while I was in the shower, God said, "I didn't create you to be an angel. I created you to be a human being with weaknesses to give to me so I can perfect them!"

God sees when we get bent out of shape. He knows how we will react to the trials in our life and how we will hold up under pressure. He knows when we will be stuck between belief and unbelief and hold onto our doubts because our situations look so impossible! He sees the ugliness in our hearts. He knows there will be times when we deny him and follow ourselves and others. He sees when we begin to run away from Him instead of running to His loving arms!

"Where could I go from your spirit?" Or where could I flee from your presence?" (Psalm 139:7 NIV)

"O Lord you have searched me (thoroughly) and have known me. You know my sitting down and my uprising. You understand my thoughts afar off. You sift and search out my path and my lying down, and you are acquainted with all my ways. For there is not a word in my tongue (still unuttered), but, behold, O Lord. You know it altogether." (Psalm 139:1-4 AMP)

So, think of this! Even though God sees all and knows all about us, He loves us without any conditions. We don't have to perform for His love. If we deny Him, He never leaves or forsakes us. When we look anything but the reflection of Jesus, He sees us as the apple of His eye! Are you pursuing perfection or reflection? When I look at all of my flaws and imperfections physically, emotionally and spiritually, my focus is on **my** appearance. However, when I give Him all of my flaws and imperfections, my focus is on **His** appearance!

When we allow the Holy Spirit to take residence in our hearts, He begins to show us the hardness in our hearts that have come from sitting in a dark room of negativity in our minds and emotions. His light begins to shine and we no longer remain in the darkness of pain and suffering! He takes us through the trials in our lives and we begin to recognize the power that is within us and begin to draw from His deep well of love. When we have not allowed Him to take that residence in our hearts, we have no well to draw from and no power within to fight the enemy of our souls!

Residence means the fact of being officially present. (Funk and Wagnall)

Is the Holy Spirit officially present in your heart? If you have accepted Him into your heart, are you drawing from His deep well of love within you? Do you recognize the power within you?

One day the Lord spoke this into my heart. "Many of my children do not recognize my resurrection power that is within them. I am going to teach you more of my power in you. As you begin to recognize my power your faith will become stronger. Without my power my children are like dead batteries. When they connect to me I charge them up. My children can do nothing without my power. My power enables you to resist the devil of all his schemes. When you spend time with me you receive my energy to do my will for your life. My power brings joy to your life and in turn you take that joy to others. When a battery is turned on there is life. When you are turned on to my spirit your spirit becomes alive. Without my power there is no light and you remain in the darkness. I turn on the light of your spirit!"

Without a personal relationship with God we are lifeless. When we allow Him to work in our hearts, He changes us and we become a reflection of Him!

For many years I taught decorating and sold decorative accessories. I loved the challenge of beautifying women's homes and watching the excitement in their faces as we would work together to build a grouping on their walls or tables. As I entered their homes, I would experience their love of nature, animals, country settings, and dreams of exciting places with vibrant colors or subdued earth tones. I would feel the charm of markets with rustic baskets and the beauty of fresh flowers and plants. I would view exquisite detail in their décor of country, traditional, contemporary or modern. My favorite decorative accessory was a mirror. Even though it was such an extraordinary piece, the beauty was enhanced when I would place the candles, figurines, flowers or plaques in front to reflect the light and color around it.

However, before the candles were lit, you could see the reflection but it wasn't radiant.

Radiant is to give back an image of, to cause as a result of ones actions, character to manifest as the result of influence, imitation. (Funk and Wagnall)

"And we who with unveiled faces all reflect the Lord's glory, are being transformed into His likeness with ever increasing glory which comes from the Lord, who is the Spirit." (II Corinthians 3:18 NIV)

It's so easy for a Christian to reflect Jesus when everything is going great. But how do we reflect Jesus when we are going through a trial? I am reminded of a precious lady in our church. Her husband died on Christmas night after an illness of three and one half years. On Christmas morning we received a phone call from her that my husband and I will never forget!

She asked us with excitement in her voice if we had heard the good news! Then she told us that her husband went home the night before to be with Jesus! At the funeral she wore a red dress and was consoling all of us who loved them. I remember how radiant she looked and realized that she was a reflection of Jesus!

When candles are lit they produce a fire that brings radiance in the mirror. As we experience a fiery trial holding Jesus' hand we become a radiant reflection of Him. Our precious friend had a hold of Jesus' hand and didn't let go!

One day as my husband and I were praying……….he said, "Lord you bring us tweaks in our life to cause us to draw to you even more."

A tweak means to pinch or twist sharply. (Funk and Wagnall)

OUCH!!!! Sometimes we do have tweaks or terrible storms that look like they will never end and trials that last for years on end and we can't see the finish!

What does God want to teach us? Will you let Him light the candle of your spirit and be transformed or will you sink into despondency and not respond to God's love?

Despondency is dejected in spirit from loss of hope or courage; disheartened. (Funk and Wagnall)

Did you know that when you light a candle in the bathroom, it helps to keep the bathroom mirror from getting steamed up? How do you keep from getting steamed up over situations? I heard a statement …….. "Anger can do more harm to the vessel in which it is stored than anything on which it is poured!"

"A fool gives full vent to his anger but a wise man keeps himself under control." (Proverbs 29:11 NIV)

When you vent your anger against others it produces strife and allows the enemy to place guilt and condemnation.

You can't fight fire with fire. It takes a lot of water to put a fire out! So it is with anger. Angry words only fuel the fire. It is God's word with His living water that will douse the fire.

"When words are many, sin is not absent but he who holds his tongue is wise." (Proverbs 10:19 NIV)

One day as I was praying God began to show me what is involved in the spirit of strife.

S- selfishness- caring for one's own interest or comfort

T- turmoil- confused motion, disturbance

R- resentment - anger and ill will in view of a wrong or injury done

I- indifference- unimportant, having no interest or feeling, unconcerned

F- fear- an uneasy feeling that something may happen contrary to one's desires

E- ego – pride, self centered, conceit, arrogance, an undue sense of one's own superiority

In our renewals, we have a drama that begins with a woman who has been wounded by insensitive words from her friend in church. The more she allows the thoughts in her mind and continually replays the words spoken to her the more resentful she becomes. She decides that she is going to call her friend on the phone to give her a piece of her mind! However, she knows the right thing to do is to feed her spirit and not cater to her flesh. The spirit of confusion is present as she picks up her Bible with the Armor of God surrounding her while she dials the phone receiving a busy signal. She begins to spew words of judgment and criticism about the other woman with no feelings of concern for her which invites the spirit of strife to come in. She continues in this state of confusion between picking up her Bible and the phone. The phone remains busy which causes her to look to God's word. His word begins to dispel her words of anger and selfishness and protects her from the enemy. Finally, His word brings humility and peace as she chooses forgiveness. The pain begins to dissipate and she can now worship God with her heart and not just lip service.

"Do nothing from factional motives, (through contentiousness, strife, selfishness, or for unworthy ends) or prompted by conceit and empty arrogance. Instead in the true spirit of humility (lowliness of mind) let each regard the others as better than and superior to himself (thinking more highly of one another than you do of yourselves)." (Philippians 2:3 AMP)

Whoa! That's a tall order, isn't it? So, how do we regard others more important than ourselves?

One day I was upset with my husband and told him off. I walked out into the kitchen and the Lord said, "Jesus attacked the sin..........not the character!" I had to swallow my pride, eat humble pie and tell my husband I was sorry.

"The tongue has the power of life and death, and those who love it will eat its fruit." (Proverbs 18:21 AMP)

When I attacked my husband's character, I spoke words of death to his spirit. However, when I attacked the sin by giving it to Jesus, He gave me words of life to speak to my husband's spirit!

So, how do we attack the sin? I repented and asked the Lord how to attack the sin. He told me to look at the good and He would deal with the bad when I give it to Him!

I had a vision of Jesus with a husband and wife on opposite sides of Him. The wife was speaking to Jesus and the husband was smiling. She wasn't spewing out words of anger to her husband but was asking Jesus to help her emotionally. Jesus was working in the husband's heart as the wife was choosing to give her emotions to Jesus.

"A word fitly spoken and in due season is like apples of gold in settings of silver." (Proverbs 25:11 AMP)

The Servant of God says, "The Lord God has given me the tongue of a disciple and of one who is taught, that I should know how to speak a word in season to him who is weary. He wakens me morning by morning. He wakens my ear to hear as a disciple (as one who is taught)." (Isaiah 50:4 AMP)

When we speak angry words out of emotion we allow the enemy to take control of our mouth. When we give our emotions to God and ask for His words and timing..............we allow God to control us! God is our teacher and we are His students attending classes daily! God never expels us from His school, however, it's our choice to attend or cut classes!

Proverbs 27:19 says, "As water reflects a face, so a man's heart reflects the man." (NIV)

One day as I was praying, the Lord spoke this in my heart. "Take your candle and go light a fire in the hearts of my children. I am the candle inside you that will continue to burn brightly as you spend time with me. My candle is in all of my creation but many are not lit therefore their spirits are in darkness."

"The spirit of man is the lamp of the Lord, searching all the inner depths of his heart." (Proverbs 20:27NKJ)

The Hebrew meaning for lamp is candle; to glisten or light. (Strongs)

One night I had a dream. I heard voices crying out for help but I couldn't see them. As I tried to follow their voices I came upon **five** pits in the ground. I went to each one but I could only see complete darkness, however, I continued to hear each individual crying for help. I tried to help them but they seemed locked in a pit that was so deep that there was no way I could reach them. I finally was so distraught over not being able to help them that I sat down and wept! Suddenly I knew what to do. I knew that if I went to Jesus He would have the key to free them. I went to Jesus and He handed me the key. I went back to each pit and placed the key in the locks and immediately the people were free!

"I will give you the keys of the kingdom of heaven, and whatever you bind (declare to be improper and unlawful) on earth must be what is already bound in heaven; and whatever you loose (declare lawful) on earth must be what is already loosed in heaven." (Matthew 16:19AMP)

When we declare God's word over our unsaved loved ones, we bind the enemy's hold on them and loose God's power to free them from the pit of darkness.

I looked up the Bible meaning of the number five. I found that it was the grace of God's goodness! It is by God's grace that we are saved.

"For it is by free grace (God's unmerited favor) that you are saved (delivered from judgment and made partakers of Christ's salvation) through your faith. And this salvation is not of yourselves (of your own doing, it came not through your own striving) but it is the gift of God." (Ephesians 2:8 AMP)

God lifted those prison bars and gave us a way of escape to get out of jail free by giving us the gift of Jesus, His Son.

"The son is the radiance of God's glory and the exact representation of His being sustaining all things by His powerful word. After He had provided purification for sins He sat down at the right hand of the Majesty in heaven." (Hebrews 1:3 NIV)

One day as I was talking with the Lord, I felt an overwhelming sadness come upon me. He said, "You feel my tears of disappointment when my children do not have faith in my promises for them. I watch my children give up on their miracles and lose hope that I will change their lives. If only they would continue to touch me daily they would find the strength from me to hold on. As a father watches his children take the wrong path he is saddened. This is how I feel when I see my children discouraged and in despair that causes them to lose hope in me. They don't realize that if they would talk with me about their feelings and emotions daily, I would touch them in ways that they couldn't imagine! I wait day after day for them to sit on my lap but many are so absorbed in the busyness of life that they have no time for me. My children look to others to comfort and fill their needs but they find no fulfillment. They become more wounded by the insensitivity of others and blame me for their problems. They do not acknowledge the pain to me therefore; they walk this valley of trials alone. They do not understand that I am beside them and will never leave or forsake them. Many of my children think they are waiting on me, yet I am waiting on them! When my children cry, I cry with them. My hands are tied until they lay all their burdens at my feet. Then I can make the impossible into my possibilities!"

So, what does believing God's word accomplish? His words enable our spirits to rise up and become strong to fight the enemy.

"I rise before dawn and cry for help. I have put my hope in your word." (Psalm 119:147 NIV)

His words direct you on His path and not your own.

Whether you turn to the right or to the left your ears will hear a voice behind you saying, "This is the way, walk in it." (Isaiah 30:21 NIV)

His words cause you to rejoice when the situation remains unchanged.

"I rejoice at your word as one who finds great treasure." (Psalm 119:162 NKJ)

Treasure is riches accumulated or possessed; one who is regarded as valuable, precious or rare.(Funk and Wagnall)

Where is your treasure?

One day the Lord spoke this in my heart, "My people would love me if they knew me!"

Do you know Him? If so, do you regard Him as precious and valuable? For many years I knew Him as a Bible God even though

I accepted Him into my heart at the age of six. I am so thankful that He is my personal God! He is the first one on my heart and mind when I wake up and the last one before I go to sleep!

When the enemy flashes his words into your mind it blinds your mind and you remain in a dark room of negativity that hardens your heart. God wants to flash His words into your mind and enlighten your spirit to His revealing knowledge.

I had a dream of standing on the waters of an ocean. Everything was peaceful until suddenly a major darkness began moving in on both sides of me. I knew that it was going to engulf me and my only choice was to go under the water! I thought I would drown! But............when I got under the water, a beautiful light was there that illuminated, captivated and liberated me! The Lord told me the next morning that He was going to take me through darkness quickly! He told me not to fear no matter what is going on. He said, "My light will shine in the midst of this darkness."

It was another process that God was working in me so I could be free. If I focused on the darkness I would have been disheartened and lost hope of God's plan in me being fulfilled. It would have caused me to withdraw from others and I would have continued to be incarcerated in my heart.

Instead, I received clarity through His written and spoken word and became enthralled by His presence as He set me free of that bondage! Praise God!

Do you need to be set free of bondages? Is the word illuminated in your heart or do you feel disheartened? Are you captivated by His word or do you feel estranged? Do you feel incarcerated in your heart or are you liberated and no longer confined. I used to feel confined and blamed others for keeping me their prisoner!

Until the Lord revealed to me that it was the enemy that was holding me captive with unforgiveness, selfishness, guilt, fear, worry and jealousies, I remained a prisoner in my heart!

Jesus said to His disciples, "You are going to have the light just a little while longer. Walk while you have the light before darkness overtakes you. The man who walks in darkness does not know where he is going. Put your trust in the light while you have it, so that you may become the sons of light." (John 12:35-36 NIV)

"Your word is a lamp unto my feet and a light unto my path." (Psalm 119:105 AMP)

In this verse "word" means the utterance of the Lord God! Are you listening to satan's words of discouragement or reading God's word filled with His encouragement? If you continue to allow satan to dump his waste, you will be buried in a land fill of emotions. Dare to take God at His word and He will shine His light on the darkness in your life! Take God's engrafted word on a quest and you will find Him engraved in your mind and implanted in your heart!

Abnormal

Abnormal means not according to rule, different from the average; unusual or irregular. (Funk and Wagnall)

My first thought was Jesus' birth. What was normal about it? It was definitely not according to the world's standards! Jesus was conceived through God's spoken word by the angel Gabriel to Mary.

An angel had come to Mary and told her that she was favored by God.

"And behold, you will conceive in your womb and bring forth a Son, and shall call His name Jesus. He will be great and will be called the Son of the Highest; and the Lord God will give Him the throne of His father David. And he shall reign over the house of Jacob forever, and His kingdom there will be no end." (Luke 1:31-33 NKJ)

Mary's response was, "How can this be?" After all she had never been intimate with Joseph, her fiancé or any other man. How would you respond if an angel came to you and spoke these words? What questions would you ask? Mary didn't reflect unbelief even though she didn't understand how this could happen.

In verse 35 the angel answered and said unto her, "The Holy Spirit will come upon you and the power of the Highest will overshadow you; therefore, also, that the Holy One who is to be born will be called the Son of God. Now indeed Elizabeth your relative has also conceived a son in her old age; and this is now the sixth month for her who was called barren. For with God nothing is impossible." (NKJ)

Whoa! Not only was she going to conceive, but her cousin, Elizabeth was pregnant and in her sixth month even though she was way beyond the age of giving birth.

Now, let's take a look at Mary's second response. In verse 38 she says, "Behold the maidservant of the Lord! Let it be to me according to your word." Do you see the faith in Mary? She took the Lord at His word and praised Him as though it had already been accomplished! She didn't say, "Wait a minute, can you repeat that, please? I don't think I've heard you right? C'mon, you want me to believe for two miracles?" She didn't say "Okay, if this is really going to happen give me a sign." She humbled herself and was ready to serve her God!

"But without faith it is impossible to please Him, for he that comes to God must believe that He is and that He is a rewarder of them that diligently seek him." (Hebrews 11:6 NKJ)

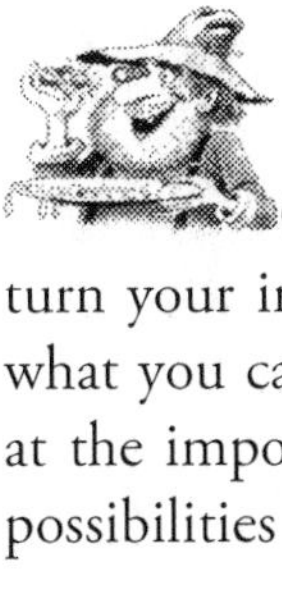

One day the Lord spoke this in my heart, "I will turn your impossibilities into my possibilities. Do not look at what you can't do...... look at what I can do. When you look at the impossible, you become discouraged. When you see my possibilities you are encouraged."

Mary knew this mission looked impossible to accomplish but nothing was impossible for her God! Some of you may remember the program years ago called, "Mission Impossible." Every show started out with an assignment that looked impossible to accomplish. During the program there was a lot of suspense in completing the assignment.

One day as I was going through a strong trial, God asked me this question, "If I gave you an assignment, would you do it?" Of course, my answer was yes! However, when He proceeded to give me the assignment, I told him it was too hard! He said, "Who gives assignments?" I said, "Teachers!" He said, "I am your teacher!"

Ask yourself these questions:

If God gave you an assignment would you do it? What if it meant giving up your hopes and dreams for the future and picking up His plan for your life? What if you had to uproot your family and move to another state? Would you be determined to pursue God's plan for your life and lay down your plans? Would you be determined to persevere when the going got tough and you wanted to run?

These are tough questions, aren't they? Yet, when we take the time to pray and seek the Lord's plan, He will give us the strength to mount up like wings of eagles and fly on His course!

One day the Lord spoke this in my heart, "Take your running shoes off and receive my slippers of rest for you."

Notice I had to give God my running shoes first before I could receive His slippers of rest! Instead of allowing my emotions to take off in all directions that wound others, I had to choose to lay them at Jesus feet and allow Him to make the changes in my heart and mind. In this process of resting in Him eventually my heart and mind began to change. I began to see Him as my hope and no longer placed my expectations on others.

"But those who wait for the Lord (who expect, look for, and hope in Him) shall change and renew their strength and power; they shall lift their wings and mount up (close to God) as eagles (mount up to the sun); they shall run and not be weary, they shall walk and not faint or become tired." (Isaiah 40:31 AMP)

Mary has heard and believed God's word and now her next step is to visit her cousin Elizabeth.

"And it occurred that when Elizabeth heard Mary's greeting, the baby leaped in her womb, and Elizabeth was filled with and controlled by the Holy Spirit. And she cried out with a loud cry and then exclaimed. Blessed (favored of God) above all other women are you! And blessed (favored of God) is the Fruit of your womb! And how (have I deserved that this honor should) be granted to me, that the mother of my Lord should come to me? For behold, the instant the sound of your salutation reached my ears, the baby in my womb leaped for joy." (Luke 1:41-42 AMP)

Wow! Remember Mary didn't ask for any signs yet God is giving her a confirmation through Elizabeth of what the angel spoke to her. But……God didn't stop there! He revealed to Elizabeth that Mary was the mother of her Lord.

Let's take a look at all of these promises of God in two scripture verses that are being fulfilled! The angel had declared Zachariah and Elizabeth's baby would be filled with the Holy Spirit from the womb and they would have joy and gladness.

But the angel said to him, "Do not be afraid, Zachariah for your prayer is heard; and your wife Elizabeth will bear you a son, and you shall call his name John. And you will have joy and gladness and many will rejoice at his birth. For he will be great in the sight of the Lord, and shall drink neither wine nor strong drink. He will also be filled with the Holy Spirit, even from His mother's womb." (Luke 1:13 NKJ)

The angel Gabriel told Mary that she had found favor with God, she was blessed among women. In other words she had God's grace. Her baby would be called Jesus and would fulfill the Davidic covenant since Mary was from the tribe of Judah and from the line of David. Elizabeth's baby would be called John and he would be filled with the Holy Spirit in her womb. In all of these promises, Elizabeth was the first person to be blessed with the presence of Jesus.

These are four promises from God that are about to manifest!

Now, let's look at the difference between Zachariah's response and Mary's response when the angel visited them.

Zachariah said to the angel, "How shall I know this? For I am an old man, and my wife is well advanced in years." (Luke 1:18 NKJ)

Zachariah had doubt in his heart that was expressed by asking for a sign which showed lack of faith and completely ignored that the word from God came through an angelic messenger. Mary had no doubt and simply trusted her God and took Him at his word and waited with hopeful expectancy.

Which response do you have when you read God's promises for your life?

Now, let's hear the angel Gabriel's response to Zachariah's unbelief!

"And the angel answered and said unto him, 'I am Gabriel, who stands in the presence of God, and was sent to speak to you and bring you these glad tidings. But behold, you will be mute and not able to speak until the day these things take place, because you did not believe my words which will be fulfilled in their own time." (Luke 1:19 NKJ)

Whoa! I don't know about you but I certainly don't want that kind of a consequence! Can you imagine........ Zachariah was about to become a proud papa and couldn't shout it to anyone? I am reminded of when my son and daughter-in-law were expecting their first child. Every conversation we had was centered on our unborn grandson. Believe me I knew every detail including sonograms and doctor appointments during our daughter-in-law's pregnancy!

"For all the promises of God in Him are Yes, and in Him, Amen to the glory of God through us." (II Corinthians 1:20 NKJ)

Amen is taken from the Hebrew word which means ***so be it***. (Strongs)

What promises haven't been fulfilled in your life? Are you waiting with a hopeful expectancy or have you given up on those promises?

On the way down to the beach one summer, I began to feel an excitement in my spirit. It wasn't because our son and two grandchildren were joining us for a couple of days......... or that we would be joining with our group of friends. There was something else brewing in my spirit. I could feel my spirit like a tea bag steeped in water waiting to drink in the delicious brew with the excitement of a little child ready to open up gifts from their parents!

During my time with the Lord I opened my Bible to Isaiah 51:3 that says, "The Lord will surely comfort Zion and will look with compassion on all her ruins; He will make her deserts like Eden her wastelands like the garden of the Lord. Joy and gladness will be found in her, thanksgiving and the sound of singing." (NIV)

Zion, a term for Jerusalem, was God's replacement for Eden. Both of them were walled in places with God's intention of fellowship with Him, free of sin, with His angels encamped around them. Even though they served idols and experienced desolation, God's heart was full of restoration for His children that would bring joy and gladness to their hearts.

One night as I was going through a hard trial in my life I had a dream. In the beginning of the dream, everything was barren and desolate. It was empty and devoid of any vegetation. It was so gloomy and dreary that I felt disheartened and sorrowful. Suddenly the most beautiful trees and bushes with the largest blooming flowers I'd ever seen began to appear. More and more variety with vibrant colors began to turn into a garden wonderland! Every inch of the land contained the beauty of nature unlike I'd ever seen and held no barren ground. There was no ugliness among the plush paradise. Everything was being transformed before my eyes. When I woke up I felt different inside my heart. My situation remained the same but I was no longer overcome with discouragement. I felt encouraged in my spirit that my God loved me and would see me through this trial.

Transform is to change the character, nature, and condition; to give a different form to or appearance. (Funk and Wagnall)

I wondered ....could it be that God was beginning a transformation in the condition of my heart.

The first morning at the beach as I was walking in the sand the sun was hovering over the ocean waters. I realized as I beheld this breathtaking sight that no matter how far I walked down or up the beach the sun hovered over me. No matter where you are going or what is happening in your life, your God is hovering over you!

"The earth was without form, and void; and darkness was on the face of the deep. And the Spirit of God was hovering over the face of the waters." (Genesis 1:2 NKJ)

"The Lord is high above all nations, and His glory above all the heavens! Who is like the Lord our God, who has His seat on high? Who humbles Himself to regard the heavens and the earth?" (Psalm 113:4-5 AMP)

Think of this! Our God whom we can barely imagine the magnitude of His spirit takes us into His account and humbles Himself to have fellowship with us!

Account means worth or importance. (Funk and Wagnall)

He doesn't see us as little peons with no significance........... on the contrary, He conveys the message in His word that we are special and have meaning!

Matthew 28:20 says, "And surely I am with you always, to the very end of age." (NIV) The Amplified Bible says, "all the days (perpetually, uniformly and on every occasion to the very close and consummation of the age)."

The definition of perpetually is continuing, lasting forever; unlimited amount of time. Uniformly is agreeing or identical with each other. (Funk and Wagnall)

In other words, your daddy is continually identifying with you in every trial that you are going through and perfecting those areas in you to bring about His completion that will last forever.

"The Lord will perfect that which concerns me; Your mercy and loving kindness, O Lord, endure forever. Forsake not the works of Your own hands." (Psalm 138:8 AMP)

Maybe some of you have felt or feel like your soul is barren, parched and dry which has caused you to feel alone. Jesus not only understands the pain inside but He identifies with the feelings of being alone.

In Matthew 27:46 Jesus says, "My God why have you forsaken me?" (NIV)

Jesus chose to take the pain, sickness and diseases of the world upon Him and became sin on the cross that day. A Holy God, His Father turned His face away and Jesus no longer felt His presence but was engulfed in all the pain of the world. Through Jesus death and resurrection we as Christians have been made the righteousness of God.

"For He hath made Him to be sin for us, who knew no sin; that we might be made the righteousness of God in Him." (II Corinthians 5:21 NKJ)

Psalm 42:11 says, "Why are you downcast, O my inner self? And why should you moan over me and be disquieted within me? Hope in God and wait expectantly for Him for I shall praise Him, Who is the help of my countenance and my God." (AMP)

The psalmist was expressing his distressed state emotionally. He is yearning for God in the midst of the difficult circumstances, yet he remained in faith and was waiting with great expectation in praise placing his hope in God.

Many of us express our emotions to others but not to God. We might as well be honest with God after all He knows everything about us and we can't fool him.

Maybe some of you have watched a television program called 7th Heaven. Rev. Camden's little girl, Ruthie, was upset because her teacher had called her stupid. As a result she wasn't working to the capacity that she normally did in class because her thoughts were on getting out of that class. Her parents went to the principal and he came up with an idea to send Ruthie to a private school where only very bright children could enroll. When her parents told her that she could leave the class, she was excited and said, "Thanks, God!" However, when she found out about leaving the school, she told God that she wasn't going to talk to him again. Then she lifted her hands up and said, "Why have you forsaken me?"

Do you feel that God has forsaken you? Perhaps you have been expressing your emotions to others but have lost hope that God will rescue you in the midst of all the pain and suffering in your life.

"Truly I tell you, whoever says to this mountain, be lifted up and thrown into the sea and does not doubt at all in his heart but believes that what he says will take place, it will be done for him." (Mark 11:23 AMP)

We can't begin to pick up a mountain and throw it into a sea. That's an impossible task! But.............we need to stop looking at the mountain and talk to the only one that can move it.

Years ago I was going through a really tough time in my life. We have a blue spruce tree in our back yard that was our first Christmas tree. One day I was feeling very discouraged. As I was walking in our back yard, I stopped in front of the tree. In front of me on a branch sat a tiny red bird. I heard God say in my spirit, "Do you see how little the red bird is?" I said, "Yes." He said, "Do you see how big the tree is?" I said, "Yes" again. Then He said, "You have me as the red bird and your circumstances as the tree."

As I have shared this with many people this has made an impact on their lives. As long as we have our eyes on the trials in our life, we will not see God bigger than our problems. When we focus on the problems, we can't see the solution. I heard a song and wrote down this sentence. "What looks like a mountain is only a hill from Heaven's point of view." (Author unknown)

Last January we were getting ready for another renewal. Ten days before the renewal I woke up with all the symptoms of shingles. Immediately I went to the Lord and asked Him what to do. He spoke in my spirit to go to a store pharmacy and talk with the pharmacist. The pharmacist told me to put calamine lotion on to begin drying it up. Two days later I was walking down my steps to check out "shingles" in the computer.

I heard the Lord say, "This is a distraction sent by the enemy. When you place your focus on me you will see this disappear. Trust me and you will see my hand of deliverance. You have experienced an outbreak in your body but now you will experience a break out of your emotions. That week three of the ladies in our team suddenly became ill. As I was seeking the Lord for all of us.........I opened my Bible to Acts 28:5 that says, "And he shook the beast into the fire and felt no harm." (KJ)

The Lord told me to stand on His healing words and I would shake this off! As we saw God as our Jehovah Rophe, our healer, and spoke His healing words over ourselves, our faith began to connect with His!

In the midst of this one night the pain became so intense that I cried all night long. I heard the Lord say to me, "You will see!" These were times when satan would try to inject negative and fearful thoughts. We had to constantly keep our focus on moving forward day by day towards our healing! As I would ask the Lord for encouragement, He dropped red feathers in our family room. God was letting me know that He was here and I needed to keep my focus on Him...........not on what was happening! My husband found the third feather and expressed, "There has to be a red bird in our house." However, he never located one! When the day of the renewal came, I no longer had any pain, the two patches were dried up and all three of the girls who had been ill were healed! Praise God! He is faithful!

Now, please don't misunderstand.............I am not saying that all sicknesses are distractions from satan. I am saying that we need a personal relationship with the Lord in order to hear His voice for our situations. God was teaching us about distractions from satan and allowed all of this illness to take place before the renewal which lifted our faith and produced the fruit of His healing power! When I shared our story in the renewal many were amazed and desired a deeper walk with God!

Paul didn't focus on what the snake was doing. His focus was shaking the viper off!

God's word says that nothing is impossible for Him so......as you give these burdens over to the Lord, believe in His word, praise Him in the midst of your circumstances and you will be able to wait with hope in your heart.

"Now we have this hope as a sure and steadfast anchor of the soul (it cannot slip and it cannot break down under whoever steps out upon it.....a hope) that reaches farther and enters into (the very certainty of the Presence) within the veil." (Hebrews 6:19 AMP)

So, how do we reach that mountain of hope? In 2003 my dad went home to be with the Lord after a three month battle with cancer. The morning after the funeral service, I had risen earlier than usual so as not to disturb my mother and sit quietly before the Lord.

In that moment, He gave me a vision. I saw a mountain with Jesus standing at the top waiting for me to join

Him. I was trudging up the mountain with every step becoming more of an effort. Suddenly, I realized why I felt so weighed down. I saw a back pack on my back that was too heavy to carry. In that moment the Holy Spirit spoke to me to unload all of my burdens. He told me to remove my back pack and take everything out that was weighing me down. I was carrying my mother who had been in a depression and had buried her husband, my job, marriage and ministry.

I had been taking ministry classes, working as a part time insurance agent and visiting my parents that lived two hours away in Lancaster County. God had been speaking in my heart that it was time to launch the ministry. I had spoken at a couple of renewals and mother/daughter banquets but felt God was going to accomplish more with the ministry. So many questions were weighing on my mind. How would my mother live alone? How could I launch the ministry and keep my job? How would my husband react to his wife being in the ministry since he likes me at home? Was I really hearing from God? It wasn't making any sense to me and certainly didn't seem like God's timing in the midst of the maze in my life! However, as soon as I unloaded all these burdens, I literally ran to meet God at the top of the mountain.

Afterwards, I watched God step by step show Himself strong in all these people and situations! My boss decided that he needed everyone in the office to be full time. I was faced with how can I work full time and launch the ministry.

One morning I was driving to work asking God what to do. I told Him that I didn't understand why this was happening now. Suddenly a truck pulled ahead of me. On the back of the cab it read ....God knows why! Immediately, I stopped asking questions, knowing that it would work out and that God was in control! My boss gave me a deadline to make a decision. When it came closer to making that decision I still had not heard clearly from the Lord. I was driving home from church one evening and was having thoughts of how I could convince my boss to let me stay part time since I had worked in the office for nine years. I heard God say to me, "When are you going to give up that job? I am calling you to launch this ministry!" I said, "Right now God!" The next day I gave my boss my notice!

Praise God! He has healed my mother and has brought her to have a good quality of life! At eighty years old, she is so active that the other day I told her that I can hardly keep up with her schedule. We laughed since we have so much delight in sharing with each other.

As for the marriage.........as I continued to obey God and take the steps to launch out in the ministry, He began working in my husband's heart. Eventually, He has brought my husband along including a team of women who have gone through trials of their own and have seen the power of God in their lives as they have laid their burdens at the feet of Jesus!

One day at the beach I took the wrong path back to our apartment. Many of us know how difficult it is to walk in the sand. Well, the path I took was longer than the one I had originally taken to the beach. As I was walking I realized I had made it much harder for myself in taking the wrong path. The sand was so hot even though I had my sandals on. Every step I took, I experienced burning sand touching my feet. I told myself, "You sure are making this hard for yourself!"

In that instant, I heard God say, "This is what my children do! I have chosen an easier path for them but they insist on taking their own path which is much harder without me."

My husband and I spent an evening at the Grange Fair in Centre County, PA. The next morning I woke up with pain in my neck and left shoulder. Thinking that I had probably slept in a certain position that caused it, I thanked the Lord for His healing power, quoted God's promises of healing, and applied soothing medicine on the painful areas. However, by the evening the pain had not dissipated. During the night I kept hearing over and over in my spirit the words, "Pain in the neck!" I woke up realizing that God was speaking to me and was going to teach me in the midst of this. He reminded me of how I had unloaded things in my purse so I wouldn't have to carry a heavy load on my shoulder at the fair, however; I left some items remain. I brought a sweater in case it would become chilly in the evening. Instead of wrapping it around my waist I tied it around my purse. To top it off I placed my arm on my purse to hold onto the sweater. I realized that I was carrying too much weight that was pulling down my shoulder and neck, resulting in pain and discomfort the next morning!

We've all heard the statement of someone or something being a pain in the neck. Yet, where do we carry this pain? The irony of this is that I unloaded my purse to make it lighter and selected what I would keep. Then I loaded it with my sweater and held onto it. I did all of this without realizing the load I was carrying. What a no brainier! Yet, God reminded me of what His children do with their burdens. We unload some of the burdens to God but keep some hidden in the secret closets of our hearts. Then since life happens daily, we pick up more burdens that we aren't aware of and stuff them on top pushing the other burdens into the depths of our hearts that become rooted. No wonder some Christians walk around with stooped shoulders dragging their feet daily.

As I was writing this message I was having a hard time moving my head to the left and right because of the pain. I could look up but it took more effort. However, I looked down with much less effort. So, what causes us to look away from having fellowship with other people and God? The burdens in our hearts become too heavy and too painful which cause us to lose hope in ourselves, other people and most of all in God!

"Hope deferred makes the heart sick, but when the desire is fulfilled, it is a tree of life." (Proverbs 13:12 AMP)

The meaning of deferred is with benefits or payments held back for a specific time. (Funk and Wagnall)

"Blessed be the Lord who daily loads us with His benefits, The God of our salvation." (Psalm 68:19 NKJ)

So, think of this! Who is holding back the benefits, God or us? I have heard many people say they are waiting on God however; I believe that God is waiting on us more than we are waiting on Him! When I worked as an insurance agent my boss offered me certain benefits. One of those was a week's vacation after I worked one year. After the first year I was entitled to two weeks. It was my responsibility to sign up for the weeks that I wanted so he could complete his schedule. If I didn't give him enough notice I wasn't able to have the weeks that I desired. In other words, if I didn't communicate with my boss then he couldn't give me my desired weeks of paid vacation. So it is with God, if we don't believe that He daily carries us and trust Him with laying down our burdens so He can bear them, we won't receive what God has to offer us.

"Whatever you ask for in prayer believe (trust, and be confident) that it is granted to you and you will get it." (Mark 11:24 AMP)

But you say, "Jenny, I've prayed for my spouse's salvation for twenty years and it hasn't happened. They still continue on their own path." God's promises don't give a length of time to accomplish His purpose and plans for our lives. Whether you have children taking the wrong road to addictions, have lost loved ones through death or divorce, have experienced betrayal by a Christian friend, or are going through a financial crisis, God's word never changes!

Life comes at us fast but God sticks closer than a brother!

"A man of many companions may come to ruin but there is a friend who sticks closer than a brother."(Proverbs 18:24 NIV)

In other words, no matter what curves life throws your way God is the best friend you will ever have."

"By faith Abraham when he was tested, offered up Isaac and he that had received the promises offered up his only begotten son." (Hebrews 11:17NKJ)

Faith is tested when everything ahead looks dark. When all you see is obstacles rest assured that your God is in control. But how can He be in control of all this suffering? Let me encourage you that God has a plan and He will bring you through this if you trust Him.

"When you pass through the water, I will be with you, and through the rivers, they will not overwhelm you. When you walk through the fire you will not be burned or scorched, nor will the flame kindle upon you." (Isaiah 43:2 AMP)

Does that mean that there will be no suffering? No, it means that God will be with you in the suffering. Whenever I've walked through valleys in my life, God has always blessed me with His presence in ways that are impossible to comprehend. Can you imagine Abraham waiting and believing for a son for over twenty five years? Think about all the anticipation in knowing that God said he was called to be the father of many nations? Abraham received God's spoken word but had to wait for the promise! In Genesis it says, "In the beginning, God."

God specializes in hopeless situations. Jesus waited for Lazarus to die. He could have gone earlier and touched him but He chose to wait. When we are in a waiting period, our faith is tried. Are we still going to love and trust God even if it doesn't turn out the way we want it?

In August 2005 my friend was in the last stages of ovarian cancer, one of the ladies on our team received word that she had cancer in three of the six lymph nodes tested along with the lump that was removed from her breast and a little boy had a tumor growing in his brain. Then, I received a call from my mother that my brother had a tumor around the stomach that was attached to the pancreas and the liver. What could I do? What could I say to all these hurting people? In my mind, I wanted to scream and say, "I hate Cancer!"

Later we were told that the cancer in my brother was so rare that there was no cure for it. Only seventy in the world have had it and they all lived less than one year! How could this happen? My brother, who was in the best health, was now among the seventy in the world with a very rare cancer.

On Sept. 3, I received a call from my friend's husband that her suffering was over! Her favorite hymn was "A mighty fortress is our God!" Part of the fourth stanza says............"The Spirit and the gifts are ours through Him who with us sideth. Let good and kindred go. This mortal life also; the body they may kill God's truth abideth still. His kingdom is forever." (Lyrics by Martin Luther)

Her life on earth is finished but her new eternal life is just beginning!

Many of you have lost loved ones through death and ask the questions, "God, where are you in the midst of all this suffering?" Let me assure you that even if you don't feel His presence, He is there holding your hand while the darkness is around you. Hebrews 13:5 says that God will never leave us or forsake us.

Just as my friends and family were on a journey of pain and suffering, I too was about to embark on a journey of knowing God in a much deeper way by letting go of my expectations and letting God place His expectations in my heart.

I started writing this message when my friend was having great results with the chemotherapy and things were really looking good. At the end of April she gave a testimony at one of our renewals on how God was taking her through this trial. Little did I know that I was about to lay my own Isaacs on the altar!

One night as I was sleeping, God told me to lay my brother on the altar. He asked me if my brother would be better off with Him or here on earth. What could I say to that?

I had prayed for my brother's salvation for many years and in his last years he had accepted Jesus into his heart. I knew that my brother was better off with Him and God was telling me to let him go! Our pastor says that everyone wants to go to heaven but no one wants to go now!

Now my faith was really being tested. Would I let my brother on the altar or take him back? I knew that it wasn't impossible for God to touch, heal and restore my brother's health. After all, I've seen God move in miraculous ways in other people and in myself and I believe the scriptures and meditate on His word daily. But, I also knew that in Matthew 26:39 Jesus prayed in the garden and asked God to remove the cup of suffering. However, His primary goal was to please His Father. Therefore, He chose to do His Father's will and not His own. Was I going to trust God that He knew what was best for my brother more than I did?

"Many are the plans in a man's heart but it is the Lord's purpose that prevails." (Proverbs 19:21 NIV)

Of course, my will was for my brother to be healed. After all, he was fifty three years old with a wife and two children, ages sixteen and ten. In my human understanding doesn't that seem like the best plan, to heal him miraculously? After all, God would receive the glory since the eight groups of doctors didn't have any answers!

Abraham's obedience to His God brought a blessing of a son that God had promised. Now God was asking Abraham the ultimate sacrifice, to place his son on the altar. He was the son that would make him the father of many nations and the son that he waited for and believed for and loved so much.

As I laid my brother on the altar with good intentions of keeping him there, many times in the next three months I snatched him back and couldn't let go! Someone said that suffering is a fertilizer to the roots of character. The great object of this life is to develop the character of Jesus. In this process I experienced a deeper grief than I'd ever thought existed! I'd been through many trials but not like this one. After all, this was my baby brother.

God showed me a dark tunnel with me crawling through on my stomach. It was so narrow that I couldn't sit or stand. I knew there was light at the end of the tunnel but I couldn't see it yet.

I had wanted a closer relationship with my brother for years but we lived two hours apart and the busyness of our lives took precedence. In his last three months we were together more than we had been in three years. We said the words, "I love you," "you're special to me and always will be" and "forgive me for not making the time for us." We hugged, kissed, prayed and held hands together.

On November 26, 2005 my brother's journey of life ended and Jesus came to resuscitate his spirit with a new eternal life of no more pain or suffering. One week before he died, I had been sitting by his bed. The radio was playing the song, "I'll be home for Christmas." I knew God was calling him home to celebrate Jesus birth along with my dad, my friend and other loved ones.

God is asking all of us as His children to lay down anyone or anything that hinders our walk with God. When we give our plan to God then we can truly experience His plan for our lives and our loved ones. My brother donated his body to science. He said, "Maybe something good can come from my death."

At the memorial service his pastor read this:

"What cancer can't do......it cannot cripple love, it cannot shatter hope, it cannot corrode faith, it cannot destroy peace, it cannot kill friendship, it cannot suppress memories, it cannot silence courage, it cannot invade the soul, it cannot steal eternal life, and it cannot conquer the spirit." (author unknown)

My brother and my friend had more love, more hope, more faith, more peace, more friends, more memories, and more courage because they didn't let go of Jesus' hand. If you are in a grieving process, you are not walking this alone. Jesus is right beside you and He understands and sees the pain in your heart. He is your strength. Give all of your pain to Him and let Him heal you. God will do wonders with a broken heart when you give Him the pieces. There is a light at the end of the tunnel! When I finally left my brother on the altar and trusted God no matter what, I experienced His light and the gift of understanding other's deep grief. I praise God for His love and faithfulness in the midst of this trial.

Let's go back to Jesus' life. When His disciples abandoned him instead of praying………He didn't take it as a rejection on Himself but knew what temptations they would be under if they didn't stay awake and pray.

Reject is to cast away, worthless, discard, to refuse to accept or recognize. (Funk and Wagnall)

As I was praying with a lady, the Lord showed me a picture of her heart. In the middle I saw the word rejection. The area was a large piece of her heart that was causing darkness in her life.

Maybe you have been rejected at one time or another by a close friend, spouse, or family member. When we aren't healed of rejection, it affects our life everyday and causes us to project it on other people

When I was twelve years old I found out that my dad wasn't my birth father. To be honest with you, I don't even know what I felt because I believe I internalized it. I didn't understand or know how to sort out my feelings. When my brother heard this, he said, "You're not my sister."

In 1998 I began to sell skin care items and cosmetics. After the meetings with the women, I found myself crying and couldn't understand why. One evening I really cried out to God. I had enough of the tears and not understanding why! God spoke in my heart that I was afraid of being rejected. I knew it was God because there was no other explanation. I began to pray for God to heal me.

A situation happened in my life that really wounded me and I asked God why again. He said, "I'm using this to heal you of rejection." I begged God to heal me and set me free of this rejection. I literally lay on the floor and asked God to kill everything inside of me that wasn't pleasing to Him. He showed me that I had a root to this rejection. The root was my birth father. I had believed he didn't want me. I told God that I forgave my birth father for rejecting me. God began to place a desire in me to locate his family. It was time to find out the answer to my question all these years. Why didn't he want me?

I knew that he had died since I overheard my mother and aunt discussing his death but I wasn't sure what year it was. Through a series of events, I located his obituary. One evening I was talking on the phone to a friend who lived near some relatives of his. I asked her to look in her phone book for any of his relatives. She found one of my cousins. After making some calls, I discovered that my step brothers were not ready to talk with me.

Another year went by till I received a phone call from one of the step brothers inviting my husband and me for dinner. During the visit I knew that his mother was not receiving me and that she said I wasn't his daughter. I prayed and felt to let it go. In the midst of giving it all over................God healed me of the rejection. I felt like a huge weight was lifted off of me. Even though I didn't know if he knew about me and if he did, why he didn't want me.......it was okay because God healed my heart! He unlocked that part of my heart that was in prison and set me free!

As God was preparing me for ministry, he had also been preparing me for the answer to my long awaited question....why didn't he want me? I received a phone call from a lady one afternoon who said she was my cousin. Through a series of events, I discovered that my birth father never knew that I was his daughter. I had believed satan's lies all those years which caused a root of rejection and placed a strong hold in my mind. God revealed that it was His plan to place me with my dad who raised me. He gave me a new love and appreciation for my dad that helped me to overlook all the things I couldn't understand. I no longer felt blocked from God's love or the love of others.

It's time to face the enemy of rejection! The Spirit of rejection affects relationships and keeps you from accepting love from God and other people.

Rejection doesn't stand alone. It brings judgment, criticism, and lack of self worth, fear, unforgiveness, anger, jealousies, resentment and bitterness and blocks us from feeling God's love, mercy, grace and compassion.

One day I was waiting for a friend in a restaurant. I noticed an elderly man who kept dropping things off the table. Every time he bent down to pick the items up............. I heard profanity. This continued many times. Suddenly, I heard the Lord say to me, "Tell him how much I love him."

"Whoa! Wait a minute God.............you want me to go to this angry man?" He said, "Yes!" Then he told me to write some things down and go over to talk with him. I went over to his booth and sat down in front of him. I told him exactly what the Lord placed on my heart. He was hard of hearing so when I talked to him about how God loved him, he got a very puzzled look on his face and yelled....... "Who?" However, I gave him the paper with the words from the Lord and he kept reading them over and over. Even when I left his booth and returned to mine he continued to read them. Perhaps this man had experienced a lot of rejection in his life. The word of God tells us that we're accepted, loved and adopted, but the spirit of rejection's objective is to steal, kill and destroy that truth.

"Even as (in His love) He chose us (actually picked us out for Himself as His own) in Christ before the foundation of the world, that we should be holy (consecrated and set apart for Him) and blameless in His sight, even above reproach, before Him in love. For He foreordained us (destined us, planned in love for us) to be adopted, (revealed) as His own children through Jesus Christ, in accordance with the purposes of His will (because it pleased Him and was His kind intent)." (Ephesians 1:4-5 AMP)

Jesus went out of His way to rescue us. So, how does a Holy God look at the sin in our hearts? He looks past the sin and sees Jesus who had no sin and took all of our sin and punishment upon the cross.

One day I was asking God for a revelation of what Jesus did on the cross. He gave me a vision of a car speeding down the highway. I was not aware of the car and began to walk across the street. The car was about to hit me when suddenly a man that I had never seen before jumped in front of me. I was stunned and in shock when I looked down at a man I did not know who was bleeding profusely. Why did he do it? What made him take my place? Why didn't he let me die? After all, it was my fault not his.

Picture this scene in your mind. Can you imagine how you would react towards someone who saved your life and died so you could live? You would be in awe of how someone could love you so much when you didn't know them. Jesus not only chose to take our place, He also took all the punishment that we deserve.

God created all of us with a blood supply in order to live. Sometimes during a serious injury a blood transfusion is needed since the flow of blood has been cut off. When we are wounded in our hearts, the heart becomes colder. Therefore, God's love is stopped from penetrating the hearts. In order to start the flow of God's love...........Jesus became the donor who gave His precious blood for all of His creation. How would you feel if you needed a heart transplant and someone you didn't know volunteered to be the donor? You would be eternally grateful to them. When you truly grasp His love, your life will never be the same.

Without Jesus death and resurrection there would be no eternal life. We would still be under the law and have no grace. We would receive what we deserve.

Maybe you have never known your birth father or have experienced abuse or abandonment by your father. Think of this! You have a Father who has picked you out for Himself as His own! He will never abuse or abandon you. You are precious in His sight. He has been calling out your name! You are not a mistake! You were placed here by God. He knew you from the beginning of when you were in your mother's womb. It doesn't matter how you were born or who your parents are. We all have an innate longing to be loved. Whatever you have desired from your earthly father, your Heavenly Father is here to fill that vacuum within your heart. Maybe you couldn't talk to your father about your problems...........your Daddy God is here to listen!

My cousin once said to me, "How can anyone else get through to God? You are always on the line!" Well, there is no busy signal, call waiting or no answer! He is always here for His children!

"He heals the brokenhearted and binds up their wounds. (Curing their pains and sorrows)" (Psalm 147:3 NIV)

One morning during one of our church services I kept hearing these words from the enemy. "No one likes you..........no one would care if you ever came here...........no one would miss you." Just as the enemy was speaking those words of death to my mind...........God spoke to two women to come over and tell me how much they loved me! I cried and cried as we hugged each other.

Afterwards, I asked God why I had those thoughts of rejection when He had pulled the root out. He told me that it wasn't the rejection that needed to be removed..............it was the hidden pain that was projecting the rejection with an expectation of being rejected. He told me that when pain remains in His children the enemy begins to set up many traps in our minds that cause us to actually believe those lies!

Projecting means the unconscious process of attributing one's own feelings and attitude to others. (Funk and Wagnall)

So.............the pain was unconsciously processing and attributing to my feelings and attitude toward others, causing me to feel worthless and not accepted which in turn gave an anticipation or expectation of being rejected by others!

When we accept rejection we disagree with who God says we are. We place man's acceptance as more important than God's. Our heart says God, you lied when you said that I was worthy.....I would rather believe what other people think of me!

One day the Lord spoke this in my heart. "I define you. Your worth doesn't come from what you do for me........... it's what I have done for you. Nothing the world has to offer you can give you what I already have given you. You are mine. When you receive my acceptance of you, this will bring acceptance of yourself."

Many of God's children have been rejected by others and see themselves as a reject. God made us to connect with Him. When we don't have that relationship with Him...........we have a void inside our heart that cause us to turn to drugs, alcohol, food and love in all the wrong places to fill it!

One day as I was going through the divorce I was telling God how I had been rejected. I began to feel God's tears as He told me that His children reject him too!

When we lay down rejection we receive God's acceptance of us. His acceptance brings joy to our hearts and dissipates the darkness.

One morning during my time with the Lord He gave me this vision. I saw a shiny coin on the ground. Many people kept stepping on it which caused it to lose its luster. Jesus picked up the coin and began to polish it. God showed me that I had dull areas within my heart that He would begin to polish and refine.

One of my friends had a dream. She was sitting at the table with Jesus. A large cup was in front of Him that was marked with the word **REJECTION!** Jesus picked up the cup and drank from it. God healed my friend that night of the rejection of her past.

When we feel God's love of acceptance, the self hatred dissipates. We no longer see our lives through our eyes but now see through His eyes.

When we know His acceptance in our minds, the enemy cannot torment us. We now see the light of His love in our hearts. Our lives are no longer about our plans but we eagerly seek God for His plans for us.

Now we fall into His arms of acceptance and eagerly receive His words for us daily. As we begin to receive His acceptance of our weaknesses, we do not judge ourselves or others. We no longer need to put others down with criticisms to make ourselves look better. We begin to see that His grace is sufficient for us.

II Corinthians 12:9 says, "My grace is sufficient for you for my strength is made perfect in weakness." (NKJ)

So, how do we face the enemy of rejection?

Get rid of it....... we need to lay these dark areas in our hearts at the foot of the cross. Then Jesus cleanses us and frees us from the prison inside.

"Therefore since we are surrounded by such a great cloud of witnesses, let us throw off everything that hinders and the sin that so easily entangles and let us run with perseverance the race marked out for us." (Hebrews 12:1 NIV)

"The axe is already at the root of the trees, and every tree that does not produce good fruit will be cut down and thrown into the fire." (Matthew 3:10 NIV)

John saw his ministry as God's axe cutting to the root and getting rid of the dead wood that prevented repented hearts.

One of the ladies on our team was in emotional pain that had come to the surface. As we prayed with her I saw Jesus with an axe at the end of the tree. Then I heard him yell.............. "Timber!" He spoke these words........."When I take the axe to the root, I bring closure in that area that will bring my joy!"

As long as the root of rejection remained the fruit of God's acceptance could not flourish.

"My fruit is better than fine gold, yes, than refined gold, and my increase than choice silver." (Proverbs 8:19 AMP)

As we face the lies of the enemy, we receive His truths. When we give the rejection to the Lord, He places His axe at the root and cuts out all the bad fruit so we can grow in Him.

One day I was praying and had this vision. I saw myself coming to Jesus to examine my heart. As soon as I gave Him the rejection, He immediately walked over to an incinerator; an apparatus used to consume refuse with fire and reduce to ashes and said, "I can only burn up the refuse when you **REFUSE IT!"**

So, we all need to **decline the worthless rubbish in our hearts!!!**

As we place the accusations from the enemy in God's incinerator, He burns all the refuse with His love, forgiveness, compassion, mercy and grace.

I had burned my thumb months ago. However, I didn't apply any medication to heal it. Actually, I didn't pay much attention to it. For quite awhile, it didn't hurt. Later, I noticed some pain. Certain things that I would touch would aggravate it. Then a little lump formed that I hadn't noticed before. As I began to touch it more and more, the pain increased. I realized that is how it is when we have a root of rejection in us. It stays hidden as long as no one aggravates it. However, when someone aggravates us by criticizing our thoughts, ideas or beliefs, the rejection in us rears its ugly head!

Now, it's our choice! Are we going to choose to allow God to examine our hearts and remove this worthless rubbish in our hearts.... or retaliate ....or run from people. When we sweep these wounds under the carpet of rejection, unforgiveness, fear, bitterness, resentment and anger we remain unhealed. The enemy says in our minds....."This doesn't bother you.....It's not your fault......you're ok!" He knows this blocks us from receiving God's love. When we decline the worthless rubbish in our hearts, His love permeates our heart!

Were you wounded or rejected by a close friend, relative or someone in the church? What was your reaction?

Did you experience rejection as a child by your mother or father or both? Do you need a heart transplant?

If so, have you given it to God and asked Him to heal your heart? If you haven't, He is waiting by His incinerator to rid you of this worthless rubbish to not only open up your heart to Him and to others but receive the love that God has for you!

Our prayer is that you receive a revelation today of who your Father is and what He has done for you and allow God to heal you of these deep wounds of rejection.

Nonresistant

During a session in our Sunday school class, we had studied a lesson on the intensive training that Arabian horses had to endure in order to carry the royalty of Europe years ago. (Divine Appointments II)

In 1982 I had a women's group that was dealing with depression, separations, anxieties and one woman was suicidal. I kept asking God to give me His divine wisdom to help them with their pain. At the end of that year God spoke in my heart that a major change was coming in my life. The following year God called out to me in an audible voice during the separation in my first marriage. He told me that I must be able to hear His voice and He was going to use me as His vessel to bring healing to His children.

So began my intensive training! As a horse has to be broken of his free spirit, I had to be broken of my selfish and prideful will. I didn't realize it but I was about to embark on a journey that would bring a major heart change that would change my life!

"Create in me a clean heart, O God, and renew a right, persevering and steadfast spirit within me." (Psalm 51:10 AMP)

In order for the horse to know the trainer's commands he had to know the sound of the trainer's whistle. I had to learn to recognize the voice of my Master.

"When He has brought out all His own, he goes on ahead of them, and His sheep follow him because they know His voice. But they will never follow a stranger; in fact, they will run away from him because they do not recognize a stranger's voice." (John 10:4 NIV)

During the time of the horse's training, the trainer would open the gate for the horse to run towards the aroma of the food however; when the whistle blew the horse had to stop immediately. Just as the gate was opened wide for the horse to run after the food, I had many gates open with temptations of my own. At one point the devil showed up with a truck load of promises. It was my choice to say "Yes" and allow my emotions to control me or to say "No" and control them in Jesus name.

"There is no one like the God of Jeshurun, who rides the heavens to help you and in His Excellency on the clouds, the eternal God is your refuge, and underneath are the everlasting arms; He will thrust out the enemy before you." (Deuteronomy 33:26-27NKJ)

While I was going through the divorce, I had some very difficult decisions to make. As I sought the Lord for His answers, I knew a task that had to be done. However, I didn't want any confrontations so I was dragging my feet in procrastination! One day as I was shopping with a friend the Lord gave me a vision. I saw Jesus sitting on a cloud with a huge smile on His face waiting for me to complete the task at hand. As I felt His presence I immediately was convicted. God showed me that He was calling me to this task and I would see His power rise within me. That day was the beginning of no longer seeing Him as a task master! I knew that God was looking out for my best. He was my defender and would thrust out the enemy who was holding me in fear!

The horse was being trained to stop by the trainer's whistle. I was being trained to obey my Master's voice. One day I asked the Lord why my life had to be so tough. He said, "If you don't walk the walk....you can't talk the talk!"

During my times of brokenness, I learned that God's word was true and I could trust my Master that he had the best for me. I learned to survive without all the material things and allow God to fill the loneliness and emptiness inside of me. No matter what pain I experienced God was there to hold my hand. I began to fall in love with Him. God showed Himself in little things that caused me to trust Him for the bigger things in my life.

Sometimes the horse had no food and little water for two days, as part of the training, which reminded me of my desert experience.

"My God will liberally supply (fill to the full) your every need according to His riches in glory in Christ Jesus." (Philippians 4:19 AMP)

During the time of separation, there were times when I didn't know where our next meal was coming from. In that desert time I experienced blessings in the midst of more brokenness. One day someone came to our door with a bag of canned goods and a turkey since we were now listed as a needy family in our community. My church was also gathering food for another needy family in another county. Immediately, God said this food was for the other family. Now I knew that we were gathering up canned goods but didn't know anything about a turkey. However, I asked our pastor if we were giving a turkey. He told me they were going to purchase one with their own money. I told them

God already provided it! The next day I received a turkey from friends of mine that didn't know I gave the turkey away. Two days later I received a phone call from another friend who wanted to stop by with a gift for us. You guessed it! We received another turkey! I gave one turkey away and God provided two more. How is that for the provision of God! I began to give up my plans and let God place His plan in me. I was beginning to learn that He was my Jehovah Jireh, my provider!

"Therefore I say to you, do not worry about your life, what you will eat or what you will drink, nor about your body what you will put on. Is not life more than food and the body more than clothing? Look at the birds of the air, for they neither sow nor reap nor gather into barns yet your Heavenly Father feeds them. Are you not more valuable than they?" (Matthew 6:25 NIV)

Psalm 68:19 says, "Praise be to the Lord and Savior who daily loads us with his benefits (Bears our burdens) (NIV) even the God of our salvation." (NKJ)

I was learning to cast my cares on Him and give Him the burdens. When I would give those worries and anxieties over to Him, I was daily loaded with His benefits of love and peace!

During one of my weak times physically and emotionally, my sister-in-law had taken me to a park. I was sitting by a creek feeling emptiness inside when all of a sudden a fish jumped up. Now I know that men have their fish stories but believe me it was the largest fish I had ever seen in a creek. At that moment I felt the presence of the Holy Spirit and a song rose up within my spirit. Immediately I had all of the lyrics and the music. It is called, "Let Go and Let God!"

Just as the horse had to make the choice to stop and not run after the food, I had to make choices daily to listen to God's principles and not follow my fleshly desires!

"Delight yourself in the Lord and He will give you the desires of your heart."(Psalm 37:4 NIV)

The Hebrew word for *delight* is….*anag (awnag)* which means to be soft or pliable. (Strongs)

Pliable means easily bent or twisted, flexible, easily persuaded or controlled. (Funk and Wagnall)

This is a scripture that many of us love to quote. However, this puts on a whole new meaning. In other words, if I would stay easily persuaded and controlled by God and let Him soften my heart, do all the twisting and bending in my life……then He would give me the desires of my heart.

I learned that He was my fulfillment and when I allowed Him to be the potter and myself the clay; God placed those desires within me.

As I mentioned earlier, this was the year of 1983 when my son at the age of nine developed severe scoliosis. The doctor sent us to the Alfred I DuPont Institute in Delaware. First they tried to avoid an operation by placing him in traction and later into a cast. The following year they performed a fusion in his spine. Afterwards, my son was in an upper body cast for one and a half years.

During this time I learned to trust the Lord with my children. I began to see that God loved my son more than I ever could. One day before the operation I cried out to the Lord and told Him that I loved my son. He said, "I love my son too!" At that moment I felt our hearts connect and I gave Him my son, knowing that he was in the best of hands. Immediately I felt a wave of His love surround me and the propensity of my struggles had ended.

The horses reward for obedience was to carry the King and Queen of Europe. My reward for obedience was the presence of my King!

"Then the King will say to those on His right, come you who are blessed by my Father. Take your inheritance, the kingdom prepared for you since the creation of the world." (Matthew 25:34 NIV)

In this season, I learned that God was truly my Jehovah Jireh, my provider. He was no longer a Bible God but my personal God whom I was learning to trust with all my heart. I began to see that He was infallible. I experienced His faithfulness in the midst of my faithlessness!

"But the Lord is faithful and he will strengthen and protect you from the evil one." (II Thessalonians 3:3 NIV)

He became my rock, shield, stronghold and Savior! When satan would accuse me with condemning words in my mind, God was my defender.

"The Lord is a Man of war; the Lord is His name." (Exodus 15:3AMP)

God gave me peace in my heart in the midst of the pain and suffering in my life and became my Abba Father!

"For you did not receive the spirit of bondage again to fear but you received the Spirit of adoption by whom we cry out Abba Father!" (Romans 8:15 NKJ)

I learned to sit on His lap like a little child and tell Daddy where it hurt!

Jesus said, "Truly I say to you, unless you repent (change, turn about) and become like little children (trusting, lowly, loving, forgiving), you can never enter the kingdom of heaven. Whoever will humble himself therefore and become like this little child (trusting, lowly, loving, forgiving) is greatest in the kingdom of heaven." (Matthew 18:3-4 AMP)

When I came to my end, He gave me a new beginning!

Lamentations 3:21-23 says, "Yet this I call to mind and therefore I have hope. Because of the Lord's great love we are not consumed for His compassions (mercies) never fail. They are new every morning. Great is your faithfulness!" (NIV)

Praise God! He didn't let sin control me. He had mercy on me and showed me that He wasn't going to let me go!

"Be not overcome of evil but overcome evil with good." (Romans 12:21 NIV)

Are you going through a trial, holding onto God or hiding within yourself? Are you on a path of resistance and insisting on your own way or are you letting go so God can work in your life? He proved His faithfulness to me and will prove it to you when you allow Him to lead, guide and direct your path!

Nonresistant means incapable of resistance or one who is passive in the face of violence. (Funk and Wagnall)

Passive is submitting or yielding without resistance or opposition. (Funk and Wagnall)

Do you believe that God is able to take you through pain and suffering in your life? He is here right now to take your hand and walk you through this darkness in your life. One day on the beach I heard a little girl calling to her daddy to come with her into the water. She said, "Come Daddy. Come Daddy!" Immediately, her daddy took her hand and walked with her.

The Lord spoke this in my heart, "As quickly as you saw the little girl's daddy take her hand, that's how quickly I take your hand when you call out to me. You are my little girl. I have been holding your hand through all the storms in your life. The storms are over and it's soon time for the darkness to move. You will see my sunshine break through all these dark clouds. Watch for my miracles!"

Little did I know what God had up His sleeve in the next season of my life!

"To everything there is a season, and a time for every matter or purpose under heaven." (Ecclesiastes 3:1 AMP)

In 1987 I married Fred Hagemeyer. Even though I was beginning to know the Lord and His faithfulness to me, I had so much baggage that I carried into this marriage! God took me out of the valley of sorrows and placed me into a fire and turned up the heat! It was time to meet Jehovah M'Kaddesh, my sanctifier!

Zechariah 13:9 says, "I will bring the third part through the fire, and will refine them as silver is refined and will test them as gold is tested."(AMP)

It was time to get rid of the impurities in my soul! God was about to heal and restore me in ways that I couldn't think or imagine. Little did I know that the pain of my past would be the catalyst that would propel me into God's plan for my life? He was about to take me through a process like precious metals that become malleable.

Malleable means capable of being hammered or rolled out without breaking. (Funk and Wagnall)

Are you being hammered and rolled out? Are you at the point of breaking? How do we stay pliable and workable when we are going through fiery trials?

"Yet, O Lord you are our Father. We are the clay, you are the Potter, and we are the work of your hand." (Isaiah 64:8 AMP)

The Hebrew word for *potter* is yatsar *(yaw-star)* which means mould into a form, earthen fashion, to be distressed, narrowed and straightened.(Strongs)

The chorus in the song called "Potters Hand" says, "Oh Lord. Take me. Mold me. Use me, Fill me. I give my life to the Potters Hand. (Lyrics by Darlene Zschech)

God was beginning a process that would lead to healing and restoration in my soul that would mold me into someone who would shine with His love.

"And the Lord their God will save them on that day as the flock of His people, for they shall be as the (precious) jewels of a crown, lifted high over and shining glitteringly upon His land." (Zechariah 9:16 AMP)

Have you been placed in a fiery furnace and God has turned up the heat? Take heart sons and daughters! God sees you as His precious jewels shining with His love.

One night I had a dream. I was at a sports event sitting in the bleachers. Everyone began standing up section by section doing the wave. I'm sure most of you know what I am talking about. Suddenly this neon sign came over the dream with these words:

There is a great wave of love coming to the church!

He was about to teach me how to battle in the spirit and not in the flesh! He was going to rid those impurities in my heart that would hinder me from taking His calling on my life. Eventually God would have me teach what I learned in the fiery furnace of afflictions!

For the first seven years of my marriage to Fred I was so unhappy being away from my friends and family in Lancaster County. I wrote letters to God every day begging Him for friends.

Earlier I had mentioned that my son was diagnosed with severe scoliosis and had a fusion in his spine in 1984. One year after Fred and I married my son had to undergo four major operations within five weeks. The doctors found that he had a benign tumor 6-8" in length growing in his spinal cord that was revealed in an MRI and sent us to Philadelphia Children's Hospital. The tumor was stretching his vertebras and had almost completely obliterated the fusion. We were given two choices.......without the operation the tumor would cause paralysis and could eventually puncture his lungs and take his life and with the surgery there was a chance of paralysis and remaining in a wheelchair the rest of his life.

The first operation was a preparatory surgery to prepare to remove the tumor. They cut open his side, broke a rib, collapsed a lung and took out four discs. Then they inserted a chest tube for drainage. After three days they removed the chest tube that was connected to his lung. The following week he had the second surgery to remove the tumor. The tumor was removed piece by piece and began at 9:00 A.M. till 5:00 P.M. I told the doctor he had an amazing gift from the Lord. He told us that he prays before every surgery! The third surgery was to place rods in his spine to correct the curvature. With two surgeries behind him, the third one was supposed to be the most routine of them all. However, with only one half hour left in the operation, the doctor put the rods in and five minutes later his spinal cord no longer responded. He was now one hundred percent paralyzed from the waist up. They stopped the operation and waited. Within one hour sixty percent returned however, they still could not implant the rods. Without the rods, because so much bone was removed, he would have been in a wheel chair the rest of his life. The doctors came into the waiting room and told us what had happened. They had no answers to why this happened or if his movement would ever return.

My son was nine years old when I had placed him in God's hands before his first surgery. I knew God had the best plan even though I didn't know what God's plan was. My prayer was that I wouldn't be the one to tell my son that he was paralyzed and didn't have the rods since he thought it was all over! The following day I walked into his room and all except one percent movement had returned! Praise God! The following week the fourth operation was a success with the rods now implanted in his spine.

As I look back on the events before, during and after all of these surgeries, I see how God was preparing my family for our faith journey in this life. My son made this statement......... "God could give me the next challenge. But I want it to be a simple easy one without pain!" Isn't that what we all want? Bring it on God..............but please no pain!

We joined a church in another county and I always felt like an outcast! What I was about to learn was............it wasn't other people that caused my pain. It was the darkness in my heart from all the pain of the past! One morning I attended an Aglow prayer meeting. A lady came over to me and told me the Lord was showing her I was called to this area. I was so upset and wept before the Lord! My plan was to go back to Lancaster County after all the children graduated from High School. However; God had another plan! I was honest with God and told him I didn't want to be here, but if this was His plan I needed Him to change my heart. Two weeks later a situation came up where God took the desire away and gave me peace to stay where He planted me.

Believe me anyone who was close to me knew that I was living and breathing leaving this area.

One day the Lord gave me a vision of a mountain. As I began to climb I would stop a certain distance and look over the valley. I couldn't see the entire valley at once until I climbed up higher. When I finally reach the top I could view the entire valley. In the valley were fear, anger, selfishness, rejection, unforgiveness, pride, and jealousy. I realized that God was raising me higher with Him before I could see the sin in my heart. If we don't see our sins, we can't acknowledge them!

"For I am conscious of my transgressions and I acknowledge them; my sin is ever before me." (Psalm 51:3AMP)

Years later I was going through a really rough time and made a statement that I hated my marriage. That night I had a dream. I was saying over and over that I loved my marriage. When I woke up, I said, "Lord what's with that! I don't love my marriage!"

God spoke in my heart to begin calling things as though they are. In other words my words had to line up with His heart for our marriage!

"As it is written, I have made you a father of many nations. (He was appointed our father) in the sight of God in whom he believed, who gives life to the dead and speaks of the nonexistent things that (He has foretold and promised) as if they (already) existed." (Romans 4:17 AMP)

I realized this was God's instruction for my life and it was my choice to obey or disobey.

"Lean on, trust in and be confident in the Lord with all your heart and mind and do not rely on your own insight or understanding." (Proverbs 3:5 AMP)

Do you believe that God will fight for you? We have a song in church that says, "I will fight for you. I will see you through! By the power of my spirit, says the Lord."

Two blind men came to Jesus and asked Him to have mercy on them. He said, "Do you believe I am able to do this?" They said to Him, "Yes, Lord." Then He touched their eyes, saying, "According to your faith and trust and reliance (on the power invested in me) be it done to you." And their eyes were opened. (Matthew 9:28-30 AMP)

One day while I was driving I heard the Holy Spirit say to me "***Inclination*** brings ***declaration*** which leads to my ***revelation***s that cause my ***manifestations***!"

I got an excitement in my spirit and couldn't wait to go home to study and meditate on His word!

Inclination means a personal leaning or bent. (Funk and Wagnall)

"Give ear, O my people, to my teaching; ***incline*** your ears to the words of my mouth." (Psalm 78:1 AMP)

"You will guard him and keep him in perfect and constant peace whose mind its ***inclination*** and its character is stayed on You, because he commits himself to you, leans on you and hopes confidently in you!" (Isaiah 26:3 AMP)

As I was ***inclining*** my ears to hear His words, He began to teach me to ***declare*** His word.

God spoke in my heart to take a piece of paper and list two columns as follows:

AT (situation now)	**BE** (as though it is)
Selfish	Unselfish
Fear	Love

I wrote a list of weaknesses in my life and my family such as: selfishness, fear, anger, unforgiveness, pride, disrespect, jealousy and insensitivity as the Lord began to show them to me. I began to bind each one in Jesus' Name and began to thank God daily this was no longer in our lives. Then....I began to thank God for all the promises that He had given me for myself and our family.

I had been asking God why I couldn't love the way He did. He said, "Because your love is selfish." When you ask God a direct question get prepared for His honest answer! It's easy to love the lovely but a lot tougher to love the unlovely.

One morning during worship in our church I was telling God how much I loved Him and asked what I could do for Him. He said, "Love the unlovely! As you focus on me your focus will be off yourself. I cannot work when you are trying. Give up your love and let me place my love inside you. Your love is shallow and has no depth. My love is deep and everlasting. Your love has no meaning and only functions by emotion. My love is steadfast and does not go by emotions. My love is unconditional. Your love is conditional. My love empowers you to take my calling. Your love disengages when the going gets tough. Your love runs and withdraws to your self. My love hides you in the shadow of the Almighty! My love gives hope to a dying world. Your love brings discouragement in a hopeless situation. Your love causes people to covet and envy what you have. My love brings desires in my children's heart for more of me. My love brings my children to me. Your love causes you to run from me. My love brings reflection. Your love causes perfection. Your love allows the pain to remain. My love heals the pain and restores the joy."

God redeemed Israel with His strong arms and will continue to be with His people in love and power! Jesus redeemed us with His strong arms on the cross to bring His healing love and power to us.

"Is anything too hard for the Lord?"(Genesis 18:14 NIV) Sarah laughed when the Lord said that she would have a son (at her age)? Sure she believed for years while she was younger but now she was way past child bearing years. But.......God has an appointed time! The Lord knew that she laughed and called her on it. She and Abraham were people of faith in God. Yet, this had gone on too long?

Do you feel like that?

As you heard earlier, God first spoke in an audible voice to me in 1983 that I must be able to hear His voice. He was going to use me to heal His people! My life was a mess and it certainly didn't make any sense for God to speak to me during my separation.

I learned when a word from God is given a reason is never required and should not be expected from us. So, I had to give my expectations to the Lord and allow Him to place His expectations in me. God sees the beginning to the end so in trusting God it doesn't have to make sense to us.

After I had written my list of what the Lord was speaking in my spirit, I heard the Lord say, "Now you are making war in the heavenlies!"

I could feel myself soaking in His presence and felt fullness of joy as my heart connected with His. I felt captivated with His love for me. I began to feel hope rise up in my hopeless situations and felt Him beginning to chisel away at the darkness. I knew that God had come to my rescue and was about to show me things hidden in my heart and mind.

"Call unto me and I will show you great and mighty things fenced in and hidden, which you do not know (do not distinguish and recognize, have knowledge of and understand)." (Jeremiah 33:3 AMP)

When God spoke this word to Jeremiah he was still exiled in a God forsaken country along with other Israelites. God was getting ready to bring restoration to His children. I tried to place myself in their shoes. What was going through their minds in all of those years? Were some of them living under guilt and condemnation for worshiping other gods? What fears did they experience being rooted out of their land? Were they separated from some of their friends and family? Were they holding resentment and bitterness towards the ones that had disobeyed God and were no longer alive? I thought of Jeremiah who had a close relationship with God and yet was exiled also!

Did you catch the words "fenced in and hidden?"

A fence is a structure of rails, stakes, and strung wire, erected as an enclosure, barrier, or boundary. (Funk and Wagnall)

How many of us build structures around us so as not to get wounded again? One day God spoke to me about the structure that I had erected which caused a barrier between other people to protect myself from being wounded. He told me not to settle for second best but give the offense so He could give me His best! Did you notice, He said **give the offense to Him**? He didn't take it until I handed it to Him! Have you been offended? Are there any fenced areas around you? Ask the Lord if you have built up any structures that have caused barriers between you and other people or perhaps you and God! If so, don't go another day but allow God to tear them down. He is here right now to give you His best!

"Great peace have they who love Your law; nothing shall offend them or make them stumble." (Psalm 119:165 AMP)

Satan offers us offense..........but God gives us His word as our defense!

Everyday I would seek God for His wisdom and He would reveal more scriptures to me. I learned to take those scriptures and confess them daily. Sometimes I would confess them four times a day. God showed me that when I spoke His word daily, I was taking Dr. Jesus' prescribed medication to heal my soul. In the midst of this I started to notice that my focus was changing. I was beginning to magnify my Lord instead of magnifying my problems. He became my focus.

One day I was traveling on a road going to a ministry class. Suddenly I saw a deer standing in the middle of the road. I was driving our van and immediately stopped so as not to frighten the deer into running into my vehicle. I waited and watched as the deer kept his focus on licking a substance on the road. I didn't want to be late for the class, so I decided to roll the window down. I screamed, "Hey, Deer!" However, to no avail. He paid no attention to me. I decided to move the van back and forth but still no movement from the deer. He continued to focus on the road. Finally, I said, "Lord, what is going on?" The Lord told me that this is how focused He wanted me on Him. As soon as He taught me this lesson................the deer suddenly became startled and ran into the woods.

As I focused on **declaring** God's word over myself, others and situations, I no longer came to God like He was my sugar daddy who needed to answer my long list of wants. One day as I was praying I heard the Holy Spirit say, "Give me this.....give me that!" I realized that I wasn't focused on God for who He is but for what He could do for me!

One night I was watching a commercial on television. A little girl climbed up on her daddy's lap. She put her arms around him, touched his face and said tenderly, "I love you, Daddy. I want a pony." I thought will she still love him if her daddy doesn't buy her a pony?

A lady shared with me that her little grandson was asked by his parents to make a list of what he wanted for Christmas. The little boy wrote, "No presents!" His top priority was for his daddy to spend time with him!

When is the last time you wrote on your list to God......... "No presents?"

Sometimes we come to God and give Him our things to do list. When we are finished...........we get up and go our own way. The Holy Spirit convicted my heart that day and I repented of my selfishness! I was trying to fit God into my plans instead of my fitting into God's plan. When was the last time you loved on God? Do you love the Lord for who He is or what He does?

There is a time to be blessed and a time to be a blessing to God! I am reminded of two women in the Bible.

"While Jesus was in Bethany in the home of a man known as Simon the Leper, a woman came to him with an alabaster jar of very expensive perfume, which she poured on his head as He was reclining at the table. When the disciples saw this, they were indignant. "Why this waste, they asked?" This perfume could have been sold at a high price and money given to the poor. Aware of this, Jesus said to them, "Why are you bothering this woman?" She has done a beautiful thing to me. The poor you will always have with you, but you will not always have me. When she poured this perfume on my body, she did it to prepare me for burial. I tell you the truth, wherever this gospel is preached throughout the world, what she has done will also be told in memory of her." (Matthew 26:6-13 AMP)

The spikenard oil was very valuable and was imported from India. The cost of the oil was equal to approximately one year's wages! It was made from plants that grew in high elevations in the Himalayas. When Mary, the sister of Lazarus and Martha, poured the oil on Jesus' head it represented an act of honor. (Nelson's NKJ SB pg.1672)

"Mary took a pound of very costly oil of spikenard, anointed the feet of Jesus and wiped His feet with her hair. And the house was filled with the fragrance of the oil." (John 12:3 NKJ)

Mary not only poured the oil on Jesus head but also anointed His feet and wiped His feet with her hair. Mary gave value to Jesus whom she loved and was totally devoted and committed to Him…….. Not her money!

When I was going through some tough situations in my life, God spoke in my spirit and said, "You could have it a lot worse. You could be without me!"

That day I began to realize the rich treasure I have in my relationship with the Lord. I couldn't imagine my life without the presence of the Lord. One morning in my time with the Lord I told Him that I wasn't going to ask Him for anything, I was just going to love on Him! As I was pouring out my love for Him in words and songs of praise, He was blessing me with His wonderful presence!

I heard Him say..............."You have been a blessing to me today! I love when you tell me that you love me."

Think about how you feel as a parent! You don't want your children to come and ask for things all the time and always see you as a sugar daddy or mama! Don't you love when your child sits on your lap looking adoringly into your eyes? How do you feel when you hear them say, "You are a special mom or dad and I love you so much?"

In Luke 7:38-50 a sinful woman came to Jesus. There has been much speculation however; we do not know her sin or who she was. This was in a Pharisees' home not a leper's where no Pharisee would have ever gone.

In one of our retreats one of the girls on the team portrayed the sinful woman. During our practice time she began to weep and weep. The night before the drama she felt drops of water on her head while she was asleep. We realized that God was sending His healing rain upon her. In the drama as she wiped Jesus feet with her hair, the fragrance of Jesus was in the air. Many women remarked how they felt God's presence!

Even though this sinful woman didn't say a word................ her actions showed a broken and contrite heart before the Lord!

"The Lord is close to those who are of a broken heart and saves such as are crushed with sorrow for sin and are humbly and thoroughly penitent." (Psalm 34:18 AMP)

So.............Mary sacrificed out of her love, commitment and devotion to bless Jesus. The sinful woman sought Jesus out of a broken and contrite heart and received the blessing of forgiveness from Him!

I thought about how Jesus was at these destinations in His precise timing with His divine appointments teaching two different lessons. In the first lesson the disciples saw the value in having a relationship with Jesus and what it means to sacrifice and become a committed and devoted servant to Him. They saw the compassion and love of Jesus for people who were shunned by others because of the leprosy. There is speculation that Simon the leper was the father of Lazarus, Mary and Martha and evidently Jesus had already healed him.

The second lesson was in a Pharisee's home. The Pharisees had branded her as a sinful woman however; they did not see the sin in their own hearts. Jesus separated the sin from this woman and saw her brokenness and repentant heart. It's much easier to see the outward sin of others but a lot harder to see the sin in our own hearts.

One night as I was sleeping, I kept hearing in my spirit......."Did I do that?" When I woke up in the morning, the Holy Spirit spoke these words to me, "Remove the log from your eye and I will change you! As you do to others, you do to me. When you love others you love me. When you judge and criticize others, you judge and criticize me. When you reject others you reject me. How can you say you love me if you do not love others?"

"If someone says, "I love God," and hates (detests, abominates) his brother, (in Christ) he is a liar; for he who does not love his brother whom he has seen, "how can he love God whom he has not seen?" (I John 4:20 NKJ)

Hate is a pretty strong word isn't it? We as Christians do not like to think that we ever have that emotion.

Detest means to dislike with intensity. (Funk and Wagnall)

Maybe someone has abused or wounded you and it has brought an intense disliking for them. If so, review the chapter on forgiveness and choose to forgive them.

"Do not judge and criticize and condemn others, so that you may not be judged and criticized and condemned yourselves. For just as you judge and criticize and condemn others, you will be judged, and criticized and condemned and in accordance with the measure you (use to) deal out to others, it will be dealt out against you. Why do you stare from without at the very small particle that is in your brother's eye but do not become aware of and consider the beam of timber that is in your own eye? Or how can you say to your brother, Let me get the tiny particle out of your eye, when there is a beam of timber in your own eye? You hypocrite, first get the beam of timber out of your own eye, and then you will see clearly to take the tiny particle out of your brother's eye." (Matthew 7: 1-5 AMP)

In reading this scripture, did you ever wonder why Jesus said we have a beam of timber in our own eye and our brother has a tiny particle? Perhaps as we bring this spirit of judgment and criticism to the Lord.........we begin to see through God's eye of mercy and love for others. Now we don't look at their sins because we have allowed God to remove the plank of our sins!

The Pharisees sat on satan's judgment seat and pointed their finger of criticism and condemnation at the woman and Jesus. They knew about God but didn't have a relationship with the King of Kings who sits on His throne of mercy, love and forgiveness!

Now, let's be honest. Do you sit on the judgment seat and criticize and condemn others or do you bring those judgments to God's seat of mercy, love and forgiveness and ask Him to remove them from your heart?

When the Holy Spirit revealed these words to me I asked the Lord to forgive me for judging and criticizing others. As I turned to my God who is love, He revealed the negativity that was plaguing my mind and the thoughts of judgment and criticisms dissipated. I began to thank the Lord that He had removed the log from my own eye and asked Him to help me see others through His eyes!

One day as I was praying with someone, God showed me a vision of a bull's eye on the target! I saw the name............ HIT LIST written on top of the bull's eye!

God showed me this process of declaring His word was His HIT LIST against the enemy of God's children.

"Is not My word like fire (that consumes all that cannot endure the test)? says the Lord, and like a hammer that breaks in pieces the rock (of most stubborn resistance)?" (Jeremiah 23:29 AMP)

God takes the tool of His word and begins to break the rock of discouragement, rejection and despair and softens those hardened areas in your heart so you are able to receive His love!

I can't guarantee that other people will change but I guarantee that YOU WILL CHANGE!! In this process, your heart will be cleansed and free!

I used to feel that I was in a prison and blamed others. However, God showed me that my heart was imprisoned!

One day the Lord asked me this question. How did the Apostle Paul have joy in prison? I said, "I don't know, Lord." He said, "Because he wasn't imprisoned in his heart."

In II Corinthians 12:9-10 Paul actually boasted of his weaknesses not his own strengths, knowing that in his weakness God's power would be evident through him to others.

"Therefore most gladly I will rather boast in my infirmities that the power of Christ may rest upon me. Therefore, I take pleasure in infirmities, in reproaches, in needs, in persecutions, in distress, for Christ's sake, for when I am weak, than I am strong." (NKJ)

WOW! Do you feel God's power in that statement? God had captured Paul's heart and mind. Paul was not allowing the enemy to steal from him. Paul could take pleasure and boast in His God in the midst of his trials. He served God because he loved him not because it was his duty!

As I began to speak positive confessions and thank God for things that hadn't taken place yet, His word began to discern my thoughts, words and attitudes of my heart.

"For the word of God is living and powerful, and sharper than any two-edged sword, piercing even to the division of soul and spirit, and of joints and marrow, and is a discerner of the thoughts and intents of the heart. Sharper than any double-edged sword, it penetrates even to dividing soul and spirit, joints and marrow; it judges the thoughts and attitudes of the heart." (Hebrews 4:12 NKJ)

As I continued to pray the **hit list**, I stopped begging. My faith was beginning to rise and my spirit was connecting with His spirit. I wasn't feeling anxious and worried as I had before.

We rescued a little mixed shiatsu, Danny, from the SPCA. One morning he was lying beside me on a chair. I was eating some cereal and noticed that he wasn't aggressive and begging me. Instead he continued to cuddle beside me. Since he wasn't begging I gave him a small amount of the cereal. He still did not beg for more. I said, Danny, "Do you know why I'm giving you more? You didn't beg for it." I realized that God was showing me that is what He wanted from me……. just to love Him no matter what!

"Do not fret or have any anxiety about anything, but in every circumstance and in everything; by prayer and petition (definite requests), with thanksgiving, continue to make your wants known to God." (Philippians 4:6 AMP)

I began to learn to bring specific requests to God even for the smaller things. We have a white ceramic canister set on our kitchen counter. One day I noticed a chip in the one that contained the white flour. I looked all over the counter but did not locate it. I decided to sift all of the flour but it was like looking for a needle in a haystack. Then……….I remembered that I had made ham pot pie and raisin bran muffins and shared some with other people. I began to panic saying, "Oh no, what if someone receives that chip in their food?" Immediately, I heard the Lord say, "You'll be surprised!" I had no idea what that meant except that I received His peace for the situation even though I still did not locate the tiny chip.

One evening I was having a pity party and decided to retrieve one of the muffins from my freezer at 10:00 PM. I was sitting on my living room sofa soothing my emotions when suddenly I bit into something. You guessed it! The little chip from the canister set had surfaced. Needless to say……..I was pleasantly surprised and left my pity party abruptly. I joined Jesus at His praise service and praised my God for His faithfulness and love for me!

As I was studying on the scriptures of peace, I found at least 432 verses.............so I would say that this is very important to our well being.

One day as I was preparing for another renewal the Lord spoke this in my heart, "You will carry my peace. Remember you can choose to remain in my peace or you can give it away to the enemy."

Ever since this word from the Lord.........I have felt His peace in situations that I didn't feel that I could get through. I asked the Lord what is different now. He told me that when He spoke this word to me........I believed it. Therefore, I have carried His peace!

Do you know His peace? Have you experienced His peace in the midst of the storms in your life? The following is an exercise that God gave me in my quiet time as I was listening to instrumental music in the background. We have used this in our renewals and many have experienced His peace in the midst of the turmoil in their lives.

Sit in the quietness of my peace. My peace flows like a river upon you when you sit quietly before me. My peace gives you rest in a weary world. My peace overcomes the evil darts that satan throws at you. My peace floods your soul with contentment. My peace flows into every crack and crevice in your heart that has been wounded. My peace brings joy in the midst of your sorrows.

My peace fills your emptiness. My peace stills the storm inside and all around you. My peace brings assurance that I am in control of every circumstance in your life. My peace brings forgiveness into families where there has been unforgiveness. My peace removes the selfishness and instills the selflessness. My peace brings love into a fallen world. My peace brings the desire to lay down resentment and bitterness of the hearts.

I now give you my peace like a transcending river that will flow on and on. Receive this, my child! It is yours!

"And God's peace shall be yours,(that tranquil state of a soul assured of its salvation through Christ and so fearing nothing from God and being content with its earthly lot of whatever sort that is that peace) which transcends all understanding shall garrison and mount guard over your hearts and minds in Christ Jesus." (Philippians 4:7AMP)

Garrison means to place troops in, the military forces stationed in a fort or town. (Funk and Wagnall)

Instead of focusing on your problems mounting.........see God's military forces mounting their horses and chariots of fire to give you His peace.

In II Kings 6 the King of Aram (Arameans) was at war with Israel. Time and time again Elisha warned the King of Israel where the Arameans were.

The King of Aram was enraged and wanted to know how Israel knew where they would be. One of his officers told him about Elisha the prophet who was saying the very words that the King would speak in his room. The King ordered Elisha to be found and for them to take horses and chariots and a strong force to go by night and surround the city.

"When Elisha's servant saw this army had surrounded the city, Oh my lord, what shall we do? Elisha said, Don't be afraid. Those who are with us are more than those who are with them. And Elisha prayed, O Lord, open his eyes so he may see. Then the Lord opened the servant's eyes, and he looked and saw the hills full of horses and chariots of fire all around Elisha!" (II Kings 6:15-17 NIV)

Can you imagine seeing the spirit world with God's angels all around us?

"The Angel of the Lord encamps around those who fear Him (who revere and worship Him with awe) and each of them He delivers."(Psalm 34:7 AMP)

One of the women on the team found the following concerning peace:

PEACE

P~ Purposefully
An idea or ideal kept before the mind as an end of effort or action; design, settled resolution; determination, intentional

E~ Embracing
To accept willingly to take in visually or mentally

A~ All
And whatever; beyond all doubt, whole being, totally

C~ Circumstances
The conditions, influences affecting persons or actions, a factor connected with an act, event or condition either as an accessory or as a determining element

E~ Everyday

(Author unknown)

We need to purposefully embrace all circumstances everyday! One day we were praying with a lady on our team who was having problems with anxiety about a certain situation. As we called forth peace like a transcending river to flow on and on in every area of her body she told us with excitement how she felt peace into her ovaries!

I experienced just the opposite! One day I began to have a lot of pain in my ovaries. No matter what I took to alleviate the pain…………it remained. I immediately took my case under God's advisement on what to do.

A week later I had a dream. A person told me they had a heart problem and had to have surgery but all I had to do was to take authority over the spirit of fear! I woke up and bound the spirit of fear in Jesus Name. The pain was gone immediately!

This was part of the process in rooting out the fear that I spoke of earlier in this book.

"And the God of peace will crush satan under your feet shortly." (Romans 16:20 NKJ)

The spirit of fear was affecting me physically, emotionally, and spiritually. My Jehovah Shalom, peace, moved in and kicked fear out!

"Peace I leave with you, my peace I give you. I do not give to you as the world gives. Do not let your hearts be troubled and do not be afraid." (John 14:27 NIV)

As I was spending time in the Lord's presence, sadness began to come all over me! He began to speak these words to me. "My peace I give to you. Not as the world gives but what I give in the midst of your trials. The world does not know my peace. They run around like scared rabbits in all directions and do not have any direction. I give my children guidance and direction. I remove the fear of stepping out of their comfort zones. I place my word in their hearts. The world does not hear my voice for they do not recognize me. I call to all my children everyday yet many are too busy to listen and spend the time getting to know me. How can I be their best friend when they don't take the time to cultivate a relationship with me? I wait everyday for my children to sit at my feet so I can comfort, heal, restore and teach them. I am a God that patiently waits for the right opportunity to touch my children in ways they can't imagine. When you invite a friend to be with you, you prepare for your special time. You work everything out in your schedule and make room for this special appointment. Yet many of my children do not make room for their special time with me, their daddy. This grieves my heart. I miss my time with them. I have so much to give and share with them."

I could feel the pain and rejection in the Lord's heart. God waits for us daily to spend time with him. Just as our friends would miss us if we would not be with them……………God misses us even more.

Cultivate means to care for; as to promote growth and abundance, to improve or develop by study or training; refine, or to promote the development of or advancement. (Funk and Wagnall)

When we spend time in His presence and study His word, He begins to refine our hearts that promote the growth in our walk with Him.

As I began to speak positive confessions and thank God for things that hadn't taken place yet, I felt an excitement well up in my heart! I was receiving His ***revelations!***

Isn't it about time that we take back what the enemy has stolen from us? You don't have to chase the devil everywhere. I believe that he gets too much credit and loves it. God honors a thankful heart!

In John 11 Lazarus had been dead for four days which produced a bad odor. Verse 40 says Jesus said, "Did I not tell you that if you believed, you would see the glory of God?" (NKJ)

Sometimes we look at situations and people and say they are never going to change. Maybe you or someone close to you has an addiction to food, drugs, alcohol or sex. It looks so hopeless! The good news is if it looks dead, praise God for He was dead and is alive therefore He calls all dead things as though they are alive!

When Jesus received the message that Lazarus had died, He said, "This sickness is not to end in death; but (on the contrary) it is to honor God and to promote His glory, that the Son of God may be glorified through it." (John 11:4 AMP)

As I was thanking God and standing on His word for all these situations, I was not limiting God by my unbelief or looking at things that could never change. Instead my faith and belief were rising in my heart and my spirit!

"Have faith that whatever you ask for in prayer, believe that you have received it, and it will be yours." (Mark 11:24 NIV)

"But be doers of the word (obey the message and not merely listeners to it betraying yourselves (into deception by reasoning contrary to the truth)." (James 1:22 AMP)

In praying the **hit list** I stopped begging and pleading with God to change the situation and other people. I now was allowing God to do the changes in me. God began to show me the darkness in my heart. As He revealed these areas to me step by step I would lay them at His feet. Little by little He began the changes in my mind, will and emotions. I realized that I couldn't change the situations or other people...........only myself with God's help! As hope began to rise up in my heart I began to wait with great expectation!

As I confessed God's word I began to see it in the spirit.

Proverbs 29:18 says, "Where there is no vision (no redemptive revelations of God), the people perish; but he who keeps the law of God, which includes that of man) blessed (happy, fortunate, and enviable is he." (AMP)

As I **declared** His word over myself and the situations in my life I began to receive His **revelations** and began to get finer tuned to His voice!

One morning the Lord spoke in my heart. "I am fine tuning you. A piano will not have its true sound unless the master key is working, so it is with you. I am your Master and you are like the piano. When I sit down to play the keys, everything must be in order. When I say go this way……you must listen and obey. When something or someone is not from me………you must hear my voice. Man's desires are not like my desires for you. There are many things that are good but have not been chosen from me for your life."

I began to see myself as an over comer rather than overcome by the sin. I was no longer talking about my problems but talking to the problems!

The Lord spoke this to me one day. "Don't see yourself as a victim of your circumstances. See yourself walking in the victory of your circumstances. When you see yourself as an over comer of the circumstances you will no longer stay under them. I have already planned a way out for you. I knew and have known all your weaknesses and have already spoken my plan in place for your life. When you listen to my voice you will win the victory! When you listen to the enemy's voice you remain the victim. This is a new day, my child. Rise up and take hold of the blessings that I have hand picked and spoken over you today. Give me your victim mentality."

One night while I was sleeping, the Holy Spirit spoke this in my heart, "***The wind of my Holy Spirit will surpass the wind of your circumstances.***"

Now, it was time for God to deal with my thoughts! He said, "I have called you to set your heart and mind on my words spoken to you. I am going to release your mind from satan's captivity. You will feel my touch on you even greater when this process is completed. As I take you higher you will take others higher with me.

As I had ***inclined*** my ears to hear God's word and ***declared*** His word over my life, He gave me ***revelations*** of my negative expectations and thoughts that prevented His ***manifestations!***

He gave me three steps:

1. Give God my mind and acknowledge the sin of these thoughts He showed me that I was believing satan's words over God's word.

2. Begin a word process (speak His word over the negative thoughts.)

3. Nip it in the bud...............do not entertain these thoughts.

Then the Lord spoke this in my heart. "The mind is a play ground for the devil. I want you to be honest with me on your thoughts. Do not allow the enemy to wreak havoc in your mind. When he comes in like a flood in your mind take my sword and rise up against him. When you speak my words you will have the victory in your mind." He gave me a vision of a play ground. I was sitting on a see-saw. When I reached the highest end, satan would shoot a gun full of poisonous darts in my mind which immediately brought me down.

A see-saw is a balanced plank or board made to move alternately up and down by persons at opposite ends or vacillating. (Funk and Wagnall)

Vacillating means to sway one way and the other. To waiver in mind, be irresolute. (Funk and Wagnall)

Irresolute means lacking firmness of purpose, hesitating. (Funk and Wagnall)

"Only it must be in faith that he asks with no wavering (no hesitating, no doubting), For the one who wavers (hesitates, doubts) is like the billowing surge out at sea that is blown hither and thither and tossed by the wind." (James 1:6 AMP)

So, when my excitement was riding high in the Lord, the enemy would shoot his poisonous darts in my mind that would cause my emotions to waver therefore; lacking firmness of purpose in my life.

A playground is an area used for playing games and for recreation. One of the definitions for game is a target fit for ridicule, criticism, etc. In other words...............they are fair game. (Funk and Wagnall)

The Lord showed me that we are fair game when we allow satan into our thoughts.

One day I was praying with one of my friends. I was having a hard time with a situation in my life. God showed me a vision of a hunter with a rifle aimed at a little rabbit. The rabbit was hiding behind the tree so the hunter could not shoot him. God showed me that satan had a gun pointed at me. I was hiding in fear of confrontation. Instead I needed to take the position that God was calling me to and trust God that He would give me the boldness to speak His words.

"Free yourself, like a gazelle from the hand of the hunter, like a bird from the snare of the fowler." (Proverbs 6:5 (NIV)

Satan has a plot designed to attain his objective on God's children. John 10:10 says, "The thief comes only in order to kill, steal and destroy." (NIV)

God has a plan designed to obtain His objective of an abundant life according to Matthew 22:37.......which says that we are to "Love the Lord our God with all of our heart and with all of our soul and with all of our mind." (NIV)

I believe that overcoming the negative thoughts by speaking God's word is the beginning of the process of loving God with all of our minds.

Now, let's look at the word recreation which means refreshment of body or mind, diversion or amusement; any pleasurable exercise or occupation. (Funk and Wagnall)

When we allow our minds to be fair game to the enemy and continually entertain the negativity......... satan has the victory. However, when we create a diversion of the negativity by speaking

God's word, our souls are refreshed and God has the victory over the enemy.

"For who has known or understood the mind (the counsels and purposes) of the Lord so as to guide and instruct Him and give Him knowledge? But we have the mind of Christ (the Messiah) and do hold the thoughts (feelings, and purposes) of His heart." (I Corinthians 2:16 AMP)

One night I had a dream of a lady who was holding her hands on her head and saying, "I am losing my mind." The Lord showed me that she was speaking words of death over her mind. When I talked with her, she repented and began to confess that she has the mind of Christ.

I began to research scriptures on different thoughts that were troubling me and others that I would pray with.

So, if I may I would like to share some of them with you.

Thoughts of...........the past. If you have not chosen forgiveness, choose to forgive and ask God to heal your heart and emotions.

Romans 6:14, Isaiah 43:18-19 Thank you, Lord........ that sin does not master over me, therefore you have helped me to let go of the past so I no longer ponder things or call to mind the former things. I praise you for accomplishing a new thing in my life.

Thoughts of ....needing to tell that person off since they don't have the right to talk to you like that.

Proverbs 10:19-21 and II Corinthians 5:21 Thank you, Lord......... for helping me to hold my tongue. Because of your death and resurrection I am the righteousness of you. My tongue is choice silver which has soft, clear, tones of a silver bell and I speak with eloquence which brings nourishment to my soul and to others.

Thoughts of ....worrying about finances.

Luke 12:6-7, Deut. 28:1-8 Thank you, Lord............. that as you have not forgotten the sparrows you care even more for me and know every detail of my life even down to knowing the number of hairs of my head. Therefore, I know that you have my finances under control because I am of greater worth than the birds of the air. Because I diligently obey your voice to observe your commands you have commanded all of these blessings to which I set my hand and have blessed me in this land which you have given me.

Thoughts of ....no one cares if you are alive or not.

Gen 1:27, Romans 6:11, Rev. 3:20 Thank you, Lord................ I am created in your image. I am dead to sin and alive to you and live in unbroken fellowship with you. You are my Jehovah Shammah who is always with me.

Thoughts of............what others have said about you.

Proverbs 19:2, Psalm 56:4, Romans 8:31 Thank you, Lord......... Many are the plans in a man's heart but it is your purpose that will prevail for my life. Therefore, I will trust and not be afraid for what can mortal man do to me. I know that you are for me so who can be against me?

Thoughts of ....shame. You have already asked for God's forgiveness.

Psalm 51:1-4, Psalm 50:7-9 Thank you, Lord.......... for your mercy because of your unfailing love. In your compassion you have blotted out the stain of my sins and washed me clean from my guilt and purified me from my sin for I have recognized my shameful deeds. Because you have helped me I will not be disgraced and have set my face like flint and will not be put to shame.

Thoughts of ....despair. You have been forsaken by others.

Psalm 31:24, Proverbs 23:18 Thank you, Lord....... you will strengthen my heart and because my hope is in you there is a future for me.

Thoughts of.......... being rejected since child birth.

Psalm 27:10 Thank you, Lord........ even though my mother and father rejected me, you adopted me as your child and I was cast upon you from my birth and you have been my God from my mother's womb.

Thoughts of........... loneliness, sadness and unhappiness.

John 14:18 Thank you, Lord............ you have promised to never leave me comfortless, desolate, bereaved, forlorn or helpless therefore you will come to me.

Thoughts of............ weariness and giving up.

Ephesians 3:16, Isaiah 40:29 Thank you, Lord.............you have granted me out of the rich treasury of your glory to be strengthened and reinforced with mighty power in my inner man by the Holy Spirit who indwells my innermost being and personality. You have increased your strength and power for the weariness causing it to multiply and making it abound in me.

As I began to present God with my thank offerings I began to see God's heart for me. I was focused on God's love for me instead of myself and the circumstances around me. As I began to receive comfort from His word, my heart became entangled in His heart and I began to leap with joy in the midst of sorrows. My heart began to sing when heaviness was all around me. I could feel

His love in a world full of hate. I began to place others' desires above my own and see the sunshine in the midst of the clouds in my life. I began to laugh when I felt like crying and knew that my daddy had everything in the palm of His hands. My mind was being trained to find something good and His ***revelations*** were bringing ***manifestations*** of peace, joy, forgiveness, love, goodness, meekness, gentleness and self control. My faith was beginning to connect with God's heart for me and my family.

"Be joyful always, pray continually, and give thanks in all circumstances, for this is God's will for you in Christ Jesus." (I Thessalonians 5:16-18 NIV)

When you do your part you can trust God to do His! Everyday is a gift from God! One day one of the girls in our team said, "Jenny, do you realize that God is tag teaming with you?"

In praying the **hit list** God began to show me that His arm was not too short.

Moses could not imagine how God would give everyone meat for a whole month since there weren't enough flocks and herds to be slaughtered.

God answered, "Is the Lord's arm too short?" (Numbers 11:23 NIV)

One night I had a dream of steps all around me. In the middle was a door above me that was too high to reach. At first I kept running up and down the steps continually without noticing the door. All of a sudden I looked up and saw the door but couldn't reach it. I got a table and stood on it but it was still too far out of my reach. I brought box after box and piled them on top of each other but to no avail. I tried everything that I could think of to reach this door but could not even come close to opening it. Suddenly, Jesus was beside me and lifted me up to open the door.

No matter what I tried to pile on the table it wasn't enough to reach the door. God was teaching me that though my arm was too short to reach the door of His opportunities …. …………………when I did my part, He came along and lifted me up with His strength.

You see, in praying the **hit list** we do our part and God comes along and lifts us up with His strong arms!

One day I was praying with a lady on our team who was carrying a burden of her finances. The Lord gave me a vision of her holding a basketball. Her team member Jesus was waiting for her to give Him the ball so He could throw it into the hoop. As soon as she handed Him the basketball which represented her financial burden, Jesus immediately threw it into the hoop and scored for the team. He turned to her and flexed His muscles to show Himself strong!

"For the eyes of the Lord run to and fro throughout the whole earth, to show Himself strong in behalf of those whose hearts are blameless before Him." (II Chronicles 16:9 AMP)

When we pray the **hit list** we acknowledge His words spoken rather than the enemies. We begin to wait with great expectation and become full of hope. We no longer sit in discouragement and begin to talk as though it has already happened. We become an over comer instead of overcome by the sin. We begin to trust in the Lord with all of our hearts and stop leaning on our own understanding and acknowledge Him who makes our paths straight.

One of the ladies on our team had a hard time when I first introduced her to the **hit list**. She said, "But Jenny, I feel like I'm not telling the truth!" No matter what I said to her, she couldn't understand it. I prayed for God to give her a revelation. That night she had a dream of many people who were dead. God revealed to her that as she began to declare God's word over them............they began to come alive!

One day one of the girls on our team was talking to me about her mother's salvation. She was feeling very discouraged since her mother was eighty four years old and had never accepted the Lord into her heart and was now in dementia. She said, "Jenny, it's too late. My mother has dementia and can't ever accept the Lord." Immediately, I could feel my spirit rise up and I said, "Oh no! We're not going to accept that!" The Lord spoke in my heart to call the dead bones to life.

"Then he said to me, Son of man, these bones are the whole house of Israel. They indeed say, our bones are dry, our hope is lost, and we ourselves are cut off! Therefore, prophesy and say to them, Thus says the Lord God Behold, O my people, I will open your graves and cause you to come up from your graves and bring you into the land of Israel. Then you shall know that I am the Lord, when I have opened your graves O my people, and brought you up from your graves. I will put my Spirit in you, and you shall live, and I will place you in your own land. Then you shall know that I, the Lord, have spoken it and performed it, says the Lord." (Ezekiel 37:11-14 NKJ)

She began to pray for a window of lucidity in her mother. A couple nights later she was able to talk with her mother from 10:30 to 5:30 in the morning. At one point she said, "The Holy Spirit comes down and enters into our heart (she swooped her hand)." Her mother backed up and said, "Oh, do that again!"

After showing her the second time her mother said, "Oh, you have God in your hands." Her mother listened, asked questions, forgave others, repented of her sins, believed in God and received Jesus into her heart at the age of eighty four. Praise God! Nothing is too difficult for Him!

Are you carrying any burdens? Jesus is waiting for you to give that ball of burdens to Him so He can show Himself strong to you. Have you been inclining your ear to God's word daily? How long has it been since you have received revelations from His word? Do you declare His word over yourself and others? Are you waiting in great expectation for Him to show Himself strong in your life? Do you enter His presence to be a blessing or is your heart broken with a need of His blessing of forgiveness?

One day as I was in a gathering of worship, God spoke this in my heart, "Do you see all of my needy children? When they reach up to me I reach down to them."

During a worship service in our church the Lord gave me this vision. I saw Jesus walking like it was just an ordinary day. As we began to worship God in unison suddenly Jesus stopped and walked over to a huge chair and sat down. There were hundreds of people bowed before Him and He was touching each one of them.

God is here to touch you today. As you reach up to Him……… He will reach down to you. One morning our church worship leader said, "Lord, with great expectation we come to your table. We are hungry to receive your presence!"

Are you hungry for more of His presence?

Are you ready to make up a **hit list** against the enemy that will bring God's manifestations in you and others? Satan has his hit list of poisonous darts against God's creation.........but God has His **hit list** with the Bull's- eye target of faith!

Ask the Lord to show you what is in your heart that needs to be changed. He is waiting for you to give Him all of you as you incline your ear to hear His heart for you. Maybe you are saying, "But I don't have time." It's been my experience that we always take the time to do what is important to us no matter how busy we are. Let me encourage you that as you give God your time you will be amazed how He will give you more of His time! Don't wait another day and remain in a depressed state of mind. Begin your **hit list** against the enemy of your soul. You'll be glad that you did!

Tapestry

Now that we've come to the last chapter, we've learned to receive everything we want, right? On the contrary! So, what happens when we have done all and the pieces still don't seem to fit?

I want you to picture a large puzzle with hundreds of pieces. At first when you look at the whole puzzle and all the pieces, it can feel overwhelming. You think about how much time this is going to take to finish, how you will find the time to finish it, when will you see the results of the picture and hopefully, there aren't any missing pieces. However, when you take a piece at a time and don't look at when or how the pieces will fit together, it doesn't seem so hard.

Sometimes we can't find the piece that fits and we try to make other pieces fit. We try to push it in, turn it around and even put it upside down. Yet, no matter how hard we try, it just won't fit!

Well, in our life we try to make all the pieces fit into our mold. We've studied the word, prayed, praised, thanked God and even had trust and faith and hope. And by the way God, "We've been waiting years for our answers to come forth! Where are you? Don't you care anymore? Have you given up on us like we have on ourselves? Have you rejected us?"

One day the Lord told me that patience is the key that unlocks the door to His heart.

But......how long do we have to wait? Where are the answers to our prayers?

When disappointments come into our life, how do we react? When prayers aren't answered the way we expect, how do we respond?

Some of you have suffered the loss of a loved one through death or divorce or gone through physical and emotional abuse. Maybe you have been in a serious accident and it's taking so long to recover. Many of you have suffered physical or emotional illnesses, had accusations against you or experienced betrayal from a Christian friend. Or maybe you've lost all of your possessions through fires, floods, tornadoes or earthquakes. Some of you may have lost your life's savings. Maybe you have children that have never made God the Lord of their life or are backslidden or friends and family that never received Jesus into their life.

What happens when we see our problems day after day, but see no solutions? When we see our children taking the wrong road, we want to stop them and put them on the right road. However, they say, "It's my life and I can do whatever I want to do!" What about the illness that we've lived with and see no light at the end of the dark tunnel? Will you harbor the anger and unforgiveness in your heart? Will you try to justify your feelings of rage and bitterness? Where will you place the blame? Will you get angry at God and your loved ones? Will you build a wall of tenacious pride and not let anyone in, including God? Will you stop reading the Bible and let go of your friends and church?

Now comes the hard part. It's your choice! Will you try to fit people and God into your plan or will you surrender your dreams to God and acknowledge that you can't make the pieces fit because God holds the pieces in His hand?

"Come to Me, all you who labor and are heavy-laden and over burdened, and I will cause you to rest. (I will ease and relieve and refresh your souls.)" (Matthew 11:28 AMP)

Burden means something carried, a load, weigh heavily, anxiety, to load or over load. (Funk and Wagnall)

Maybe you feel so tired and worn out with your life! One morning during worship in our church one of the women picked up a flag and her little grandchildren began to follow. Soon these little children encouraged other children to join them in marching around. One of the ladies took her grandson who was not even two years old and was the youngest of them all. She put his hand on another little girl at the tail end. A quarter of the way around the front of the church one of the older children picked him up and was carrying him.

That's how God is with us. When the trials become too hard to bear, we become weary and wear out. This little boy was too tired to keep walking and wore out.

"Take my yoke upon your and learn of Me, for I am gentle (meek) and humble (lowly) in heart, and you will find rest (relief and ease and refreshment and recreation and blessed quiet) for your souls." (Matthew 11:29 AMP)

The Greek word for yoke is zugos (dzoogos) which means coupling or servitude. (Strongs)

Coupling means the act of one or that which couples, a pair. (Funk and Wagnall)

In other words, taking God's yoke upon us makes us a couple with Him!

When you become a couple with someone else, you have a desire to spend a lot of time talking and listening to them. They are always on your mind and your heart. When you aren't with them, you miss them and can't wait to be with them again. That's how we should feel about God.

When I was a young girl in my teens, I had a dream of marrying a man who would hold my hand, understand my emotions, and see my faults but be able to love me just as I am. I wanted someone that I could share the darkest, deepest secrets of my heart and not judge me, someone to laugh and cry with, and someone to be sensitive to my needs. I used to try to picture him in my heart and I would see the way he would smile and look into my eyes with love and adoration. Then I would look at him with love and respect and the excitement of feeling his love as we held hands and basked in each others presence. In other words, I pictured a knight in shining armor that would come in to my life on a white horse and rescue me. Then we would have a Cinderella marriage and live happily ever after!

When I got married at eighteen years old and went through a divorce fifteen years later, I realized that there were no perfect marriages because there are no perfect people including myself.

But........when I come to my Father and bask in His presence, my pain begins to heal. I feel His hand in mine and I look into His face and see that love and adoration He has for me in His eyes. My heart becomes entangled in His and I hear the cry of His heart. I feel the tears He has for all the pain in my life and I realize like a little child that my daddy has everything under control. I hear His words, "**You are the apple of my eye, I will not leave you or forsake you, and you are mine.**"

As long as we are a couple, what can satan do to me? He has no authority over me because Jesus rules and reigns in my life. God and I are a twosome, a couple, a marriage. When satan comes to steal, kill and destroy my health, family, emotions, friends, or possessions he is trespassing because you see.......no weapon formed against me can prosper. Don't you know that three is a crowd?

Matthew 11: 30 says, "My yoke is easy and my burden is light."(NIV)

The Greek word for this burden is *phortion (forteeon)* a task or service.(Strongs)

Now we can take off the burden of discouragement and put on His burden of love and service to Him. We no longer have the fear because perfect love casts out fear.

Our God has a task for us. Imagine that! He knows what it takes to complete the work that He has started in us. Because we know and feel His arms around us we don't have to see the light at the end of the tunnel. We're not stumbling in the dark anymore because He is leading us step by step. It's okay that we can't figure everything out since we know and love the Master who is full of wisdom and knows what is best for us.

Now only with God's instructions are we able to humble ourselves in His presence and rest in His strong arms! We have given our demands and expectations because we know the God of the universe. We can now watch Him place the pieces of our lives together and see how it all FITS!!!!

Perhaps you are going through a fiery trial at this moment and you are saying, "Where are you God?" I'd like to encourage you that God is listening and watching everything that is going on in your life.

"The Lord will march out like a mighty man. Like a warrior He will stir up His zeal; with a shout he will raise the battle cry and will triumph over His enemies." (Isaiah 42:13 NIV)

God is your warrior! You don't have to fight this battle alone. Whatever you are going through right now, He will never leave you or forsake you. God loves you with an everlasting love! Lay these burdens down at the feet of Jesus. Give Him the opportunity to show Himself strong for you and receive His peace that passes all understanding.

As I was seeking God for the last word........I heard in my spirit the word **tapestry**. I had a vision of Jesus at a spindle with lots of thread!

I heard him say...... "I am weaving all these people and circumstances into your life to bring about my beautiful design in you. I tighten each thread that is too loose and loosen threads that are too tight."

A tapestry is a woven ornamental fabric used for hangings in which the wool is supplied by a spindle, the design being formed by stitches across the warp.(Funk and Wagnall)

As we were praying for a workshop I saw a picture of a heart with a large piece ripped back. Then I saw a huge needle that looked like a darning needle repairing that area of the heart.

Darn means to repair a garment or hole by filling the gap with interlacing stitches. Interlacing means to join by or as by weaving together; intertwine, to blend or combine. (Funk and Wagnall)

There are many of you that have a huge rip in your heart and God wants to repair that hole inside your heart by filling the large gap inside with His love. He is your Weaver that sees that hole and wants to mend all those broken pieces together. He will weave all of our circumstances, past and present and heal what needs to be healed to bring restoration to your souls!

"We are assured and know that (God being a partner in their labor) all things work together and are (fitting into a plan) for good to and for those who love God and are called according to His design and purpose." (Romans 8:28 AMP)

Notice that God is your partner. A partner is someone who is united or associated with another or others in some action or enterprise.

John 6:60 says that many disciples said, "This is a hard teaching, who can accept it?" (NIV) Jesus had already made clear what discipleship meant however; many who had been following Him were not ready to receive life in the way Jesus taught.

Jesus turned to His twelve disciples and asked them if they wanted to leave also. Peter replied, "Lord, to whom shall we go? You have the words of eternal life. We believe and know that you are the Holy One of God." (John 6:67 NIV)

So, what design is He creating in you? It isn't easy to be a disciple. There is a cost to pay in completely surrendering your life to God. However, the benefits of His love, mercy and grace far outweigh all of the pain in life.

"There is no wisdom, no insight and no plan that can succeed against the Lord." (Proverbs 21:30 NIV)

When I choose to follow God, I know that no matter what the situation is in my life, He is in control! When I release my plan and will to Him, I allow God to place His plans and will for my life in my heart. When I see and feel His love wrapped around me like a cloak, I can rest in His arms.

If I hold onto my plan, my heart begins to harden and I no longer hear my Master's voice. We can't serve two masters. If we do not obey God then we serve the enemy of our souls! Everyday is a continual process of dying to our desires of the flesh. As long as I have a stubborn will, I will never experience God's peace in my heart. When I **give up** my will, I **pick up** God's plan and purpose for my life.

Jeremiah 29:11 says, "For I know the plans that I have for you, declares the Lord, plans to prosper you and not to harm you, plans to give you hope and a future." (NIV)

We all know that we are not here for our purpose but for God's purpose. Each one of us has a map drawn out for us. It's our choice which direction we will take. There will always be consequences on the road of SIN! Most of us would like to sweep those consequences away and allow the sin in our lives. However, God has a plan to sweep the sin out of our hearts.

When we are willing to follow His heart for us, God begins to shine His light on the darkness of our hearts. We have a choice for our life. We can move towards the light or continue in the darkness. When I focus on the light, the darkness around me becomes dim. I see the light of His love enfold me.

Are you ready to give up and surrender your plans to God? Today you can pick up His plan for your life. Have you been on the road to destruction in your life? Maybe you have done something that has caused pain to yourself and others and are living under guilt and shame.

Psalm 86:5 says, "For you, Lord, are good, and ready to forgive, and abundant in mercy to all those who call upon you." (NKJ)

Perhaps you have been rejected as a little child and have picked up those expectations of others rejecting you too. Are you afraid of what the cost will be in following God? Where will His plan lead you? I can promise you that no matter where He leads if you will follow, you will have His strength, peace, joy and love. He will never leave or forsake you.

Isaiah 43:1 says, "He who created you, O Jacob, he who formed, O Israel, fear not, for I have redeemed you. I have summoned you by name. You are mine." (NIV)

Whatever your calling is, He will equip you in all that you need.

Remember the woman in the mirror in the chapter that discussed the meaning of new? Let's take a look at what design God has created in her.

"For you created my inmost being; you knit me together in my mother's womb. I praise you because I am fearfully and wonderfully made; your works are wonderful, I know that full well. My frame was not hidden from you when I was made in the secret place. When I was woven together in the depths of the earth, your eyes saw my unformed body. All the days ordained for me were written in your book before one of them came to be." (Psalm 139: 13-16 NIV)

Now, the woman in the mirror knows who the fairest one of all is!

She no longer sees all her imperfections, but knows that she is complete in Him and she is wonderfully and fearfully made.

She has allowed the Lord to examine her heart because He sees her heart. She gives up the root of rejection for she knows that God's love is ever before her and she walks continually in His truth.

She lays down the wrinkles and blemishes of her past because she knows that God has redeemed her of the past. She is learning to give the pain to God for He now bears her pain and gives her a crown of beauty instead of ashes.

She sees that God has wrapped her in His robe of righteousness and she is dressed in rich garments.

She now gazes on the beauty of the Lord and knows that she belongs to Him.

As she gives these weaknesses to Him, He sympathizes with all her weaknesses and gives her the power to overcome them.

She no longer has unforgiveness in her heart because she knows it is her choice to forgive whether she feels like it or not. She forgives because God has been faithful to forgive her when she confessed her sins.

She no longer lives in fear of the future because God did not give her a spirit of fear and she knows that God will never forsake her and will give her everything she needs.

Now, every day is a new day and she lives it to the fullest because she is glad that God gives her the joy of His presence.

Oh! By the way! When she goes to church, she now expects to have her heart encouraged by the message that God has given her Pastor. But….she doesn't wait to hear from God just on Sundays. She knows that God is her Shepherd and all his sheep hear His voice. Now because she has life in her, she now speaks words of life to others who are discouraged and empty inside!

She now has the fruits of the spirit which are "love, joy, peace, patience, kindness, gentleness, goodness, faithfulness and self control!" (Galatians 5:22-23 NIV)

She belongs to Jesus Christ and has crucified the sinful nature with its passions and desires.

She is dressed for battle, for she knows the enemy will try to bring those negative thoughts because he has a plot to kill, steal and destroy all of God's sons and daughters! She puts on the full armor of God so that she can stand against the devil's schemes. She stands firm with the belt of truth buckled around her waist and resists the lies of the enemy for the breastplate of righteousness is in place. Her feet are fitted with readiness that comes from the gospel of peace. She takes up her shield of FAITH and believes God's word over the enemies and extinguishes all the flaming arrows of the evil one. She has a helmet of salvation and opens the sword of the spirit daily to renew her mind and cleanse her flesh.

She now waits on God with great expectation of what He has planned for her life. She knows that He has plans to prosper and bring good things to her. She walks hand in hand with her Savior and praises Him for the love that He has placed in her. She knows that God has removed her sins from her and remembers them no more because of His compassion for her.

She now looks into a mirror and says……. "Look what love has done to me."

Now, she sees the reflection of who she truly is. She is the bride in preparation for her groom! She is beautifully dressed and adorned in beautiful jewels as a bride of Christ. She has walked this journey of pain and suffering in preparation to meet her groom at the altar of heaven's door.

He wipes away all her tears. There is no more death or mourning or crying or pain for the old order of things has passed away.

She says… "I am yours. I belong to you. I bear your name."

Her groom is enthralled by her beauty. He crowns her with love and compassion. He speaks tenderly to her. He calls her by a new name. He says, "I give you my eternal pleasure. I turn your hardships into my glory. I give you all my treasures in heaven."

Her husband now takes His place on the throne of her heart and says, "I am making everything new. Write this down for these words are trustworthy and true."

He looks at her and says, "It is done. I am the Alpha and the Omega, the beginning and the end!"

Can God offer life without pain or sorrow? No, life is full of trials. However, God does offer you His approval in the midst of others disapproval. He gives you peace in the midst of the storms in your life. You can have His joy that will strengthen your heart and experience His love through the darkness in your life. Most of all, He offers you freedom in your heart instead of imprisonment.

During one of our vacations at the shore I was thinking about the last day on the beach. I began to think what if this was my last day on earth? What would I do? Where would I go? How would I treat others? How would I think? Most of all, how did I touch my God's heart?

The Lord spoke this in my heart, "This day is the day to make peace with everyone. Let no day go by undone so that when your last day on earth comes there are no loose ends. I have called you to be a peacemaker daily!"

"If possible, as far as it depends on you, live at peace with everyone." (Romans 12:18 AMP)

These questions were in my heart as I mediated on His word. Will you be full of guilt or guilt free? Will you be thankful or thank less? Will you be forgiving or unforgiving? Will you have loved and been loved by others? Will you be full of pride or humble in your heart?

Will you be wealthy and never give to others or will you give and become wealthy in God's riches? Will you glory in your accomplishments or bring glory to God in what He has accomplished in you? Will you be fearful or full of faith? Have you been a loner and isolated yourself from others so as not to get hurt or did you get alone with God to heal the pain inside your heart? Did you hold onto disappointments or allow God to give you His appointments?

Have you been contentious or conscious of the Father who loves you? Will you leave your footprints or the footprints of God? Did you speak life or death to others' spirits? Were you confident in the God you served? Did you build a wall around you or did you choose to allow God to tear down the wall? Did you love at all times even when you didn't feel like it? Was your heart cheerful and therefore cheered others on or was your spirit crushed and therefore put others down?

When you were offended did you choose to clench the offense in your heart or did you open up your heart to God and ask Him to take the offense and choose to forgive? Did you weary God with your offenses or weary yourself for God? Did you hold hands with the darkness in your heart or allow God to remove that darkness by holding onto His light? Did you reach out to become friends with others or become bitter because no one reached out to you? Did you speak with your knowledge or ask God for His wisdom? Did you submit to God and resist the devil or submit to the devil and resist God? Did you choose to follow God's lead and walk in His steps or did you take your steps to lead? Did you cry with others and for others or choose to cry for yourself?

Did you take the hand that life dealt you and see God's victory in it or remain a victim of your past? Did your emotions run with your negative thoughts or did you run to God's word to remove the negative thoughts? Did you focus on God's power in your life and see satan as powerless or focus on satan's power and see God as powerless? Did you live with contentment knowing that you weren't here for your plan but to fulfill God's plan or were you always seeking for more and never having enough? Did you fit into God's plan or did you try to coax God to fit into your plans?

These are tough questions that will lead to God's plan of examinations. Now, it's your choice. Will you choose to be His disciple when the teaching seems so hard or will you take the seemingly easy way out? Either way, you will experience pain and sorrow in this life. You were created for holiness that brings true happiness of an abundant life that God designed for you. We have decided to follow Jesus no matter where that journey takes us since we know where it ends.

Where will your journey end?

So........how do we live an **ABUNDANT LIFE**?

First of all, ask the Lord to come into your heart and forgive your sins.

Spend time going to church, reading the word of God and praying. (It begins with discipline but leads to falling in love with Jesus)

Develop a relationship with the Lord- come **BOLDLY** to His throne. Be gut honest with Him.

Focus on the Lord and not yourself. Speak words of who you are and who He is daily.

See God turning your problems into possibilities! God has won every battle. He is the **UNDEFEATED** CHAMPION!

See yourself as a **NEW** creation of infinite worth!

DARE to take God at His word.

Submit to God's plan of His examination instead of self examination! Take the **ABNORMAL** journey and follow after Jesus.

Be **NONRESISTANT** to God's plan no matter what.

Know that God is weaving people, places and circumstances into your life to bring about a beautiful **TAPESTRY!** You are His masterpiece.

About The Ministry

In 2003 God called Jenny to launch the ministry and took her from her job as an insurance agent. As the years go by, God has called more women to come on the team. These ladies are not only our friends but they are chosen by God to minister and bless others and represent not only the ministry but more importantly, Jesus. We are from all different denominations that make up the body of Christ. We meet together weekly for prayer in seeking God's heart for the ministry and others. Jeremiah 17:9 says, "The heart is deceitful above all things and beyond cure. Who can understand it?" God understands everything that is going on in our hearts. He knows where there is deep rooted pain that we aren't aware of and what causes us to react in anger, selfishness, pride and fear instead of responding with his love. He has watched all of the rejections that we have experienced in our lives. God has and continues to root out rejection, anger and unforgiveness in our lives and others. As the pain dissipates, more creativity, love, and acceptance comes forth in all of our hearts. We are learning to love unconditionally and allow the Holy Spirit to do His work in each of us without judgment or criticism. Each person contributes with their creativity that God has given them and meets the needs of the ministry. We are humbled to be able to serve the Lord and his children. We know that it's not about us, but all about Him!

In 2006 Fred took early retirement and was able to join us. He has participated in drama, prayer and some speaking when we are invited into church services. He also brings creativity in making up the props that are needed for the drama.

Among all of us, we have experienced the loss of loved ones through death and divorce, physical and emotional illnesses, betrayal of others, cancer, children taking the wrong road to addictions, taking care of parents with Alzheimer's, moving to another location, and many other changes and disappointments in our lives. We are learning to lean on Jesus more than ever and know that He has the best for us! He promises to never leave us or forsake us! We believe that we were created for God's purpose and not for our own. As we lay down our plans, we can seek God for His plan! It's humbling to think that a great awesome God wants to spend time with us and loves us just as we are! Jesus didn't choose the disciples because of what they knew, who they were, or who they knew. He chose them because that was his Father's plan! No matter what has been done to you or you have done to others, the good news is nothing can ever separate you from His love! He is here with His arms stretched out to meet your needs for healing, deliverance and restoration! He never gives up on us! One day as I was praying the Lord spoke in my heart, "My people would love me if they knew me!" Do you know him?

The ministry takes the message that God wants to replace your wounds with His healing and restoration; fear with love; anger turned into forgiveness and despair turned into faith and hope! We bring you our brokenness and wounded hearts and how God picked us up out of the sewer of our emotional despair in our lives and brought us together to be used by Him!

Every workshop, renewal, ministry event and retreat is tailored by God to meet the emotional, physical and spiritual needs of the people that He brings to them! Jenny is licensed to minister with Global Ministries through the Worship Center in Lancaster County. The ministry is available for retreats, renewals, workshops, special programs and other church events. Contact Jenny for more information at www.thepromiselandministries.org

References

Funk and Wagnall Dictionary. New York: Harper and Row Publishers, 1984.

Nelson Study Bible, NKJ. Nashville: Thomas Nelson Publishers, 1982.

Strong, James. The New Strong's Exhaustive Concordance of the Bible. Nashville: Thomas Nelson Publishers, 1984.